January
Moon of the Terrible

February
Moon When There Is Frost inside the Lodge

March
Moon When the Frost Covers the Prairie Chickens' Eyes

April
Moon When the Geese Return

May
Moon When the Leaves Turn Green

June
Moon When the Berries Are Ripe

July
Moon When the Choke-cherries Are Ripe

August
Moon When All Things Ripen

September
Moon When the Leaves Turn Yellow

October
Moon When the Leaves Blow Off

November
Moon When Winter Sets In

December
Moon When Deer Shed Their Antlers

Lana's Lakota Moons

Virginia Driving Hawk Sneve

UNIVERSITY OF NEBRASKA PRESS | LINCOLN & LONDON

© 2007
by Virginia Driving
Hawk Sneve ¶ All rights reserved
¶ Manufactured in the United States of
America ¶ ⊗ ¶ Library of Congress Catalog-
ing-in-Publication Data ¶ Sneve, Virginia Driving
Hawk. ¶ Lana's Lakota moons / Virginia Driving Hawk
Sneve. ¶ p. cm. ¶ Summary: Cousins Lori and Lana, Lakota
Indians who have a close but competitive relationship, learn about
their heritage and culture throughout the year, and when a Laotian-
Hmong girl comes to their school, they make friends with her and
"adopt" her as one of their own. ¶ ISBN-13: 978-0-8032-6028-3 (pbk.
: alk. paper) ¶ 1. Dakota Indians—Juvenile fiction. [1. Dakota Indians—Fiction. ¶ 2. Indians of North America—Great
Plains—Fiction. ¶ 3. Cousins—Fiction. ¶ 4. Grandparents—Fiction. ¶ 5. Death—Fiction.] ¶ I. Title. ¶
PZ7.S679Lan 2007 ¶ [Fic]—dc22 ¶ 2007005469
¶ Designed and set in Adobe Garamond
by R. W. Boeche.

Contents

Acknowledgments vii
Lakota Moons viii

1. Moon When Winter Sets In 1

2. Moon When Deer Shed Their Antlers 13

3. Moon When There Is
Frost inside the Lodge 23

4. Moon When the Geese Return 33

5. Moon When the Leaves Turn Green 43

6. Moon When the Berries Are Ripe 51

7. Moon of New Names. 63

8. Moon When the Buffalo Run 77

9. Moon When the Leaves Blow Off 89

10. Moon of the Hats 97

11. Moon of the Dance 103

12. Moon of the Terrible 111

Acknowledgments

Pilamiye to my granddaughter and research assistant Joan Gunderson-Palmer and to Txongpao Lee of the Hmong Cultural Center in St. Paul, Minnesota, for providing answers to my many questions.

Pilamiye to son Paul for helping with the Dakota and Lakota words and with the translation of the Lakota Moons into English—he knows more than his mother. We both consulted several Lakota speakers to be sure that the translations used in this book were accurate. We found that there are many similarities as well as differences in the translations.

Pilamiye to my patient husband, Vance, for again giving support to another writing project that complicates his life.

Pilamiye to the Rapid City Regional Hospital, their public relations and marketing department, and to the Neonatal/Pediatric Intensive Care Unit for their help on children's hospital care.

Pilamiye to the Lakota and Asian students in the Rapid City School District. Their caring acceptance of each other's cultural differences was the inspiration for this story.

Lakota Moons

January

Wióthehika: *Moon of the Terrible*

February

Thiyóheyuka wi: *Moon When There Is Frost
inside the Lodge*

March

Šyóištóhcapi wi: *Moon When the Frost Covers
the Prairie Chickens' Eyes*

April

Maǧáksica aglí wi: *Moon When the Geese Return*

May

Chąwápatho wi: *Moon When the Leaves Turn Green*

June

Wípazuka wašté wi: *Moon When the Berries Are Ripe*

July
Chąphásapa wi: *Moon When the Chokecherries Are Ripe*

August
Khấta waštéšte wi: *Moon When All Things Ripen*

September
Chąwápeǧi wi: *Moon When the Leaves Turn Yellow*

October
Chąwápekasna wi: *Moon When the Leaves Blow Off*

November
Waníyetu wi: *Moon When Winter Sets In*

December
Thahécapšuŋ wi: *Moon When Deer Shed Their Antlers*

1. Moon When Winter Sets In

"Lori, follow me," Lana ordered. "Step in my tracks!"

She led me around the fence, cut kitty-corner from the garage to the house, moved along the fence again to the other corner, and walked back to the porch. We stepped in the same footprints we'd already made, so it looked like only one person had made a circle of tracks in the snow.

The first snow of the year fell in soft, fluffy flakes, making a thick curtain that muffled all sounds. We stuck out our tongues to catch them, but they melted with no taste.

Lana opened the gate but I stopped. "Grandma said to stay in the backyard," I reminded her.

But she didn't hear me over the roar of the snowblower that Grandpa was using. Or maybe she ignored me, as she often did. Instantly the blower smothered her in snow.

"Yow!" she yelled, and Grandpa heard her.

He turned off the machine. "What the—?" he yelled at Lana, who was bent over holding her hand to her face.

I rushed to brush away the snow and saw bright red spots of blood. "Ooh," I said. "Lana's cut."

Grandpa pulled Lana's hand away to reveal a gash on her cheek. He grabbed her hand and led her into the house.

She wasn't hurt badly. The snow machine had sucked up a gravel chip or twig and blown it out to the side, hitting Lana on the cheek.

Grandma cleaned the cut, put a Band-Aid over it, and then made hot chocolate for us.

Grandpa fussed until he knew Lana was okay. "I should have told you girls to stay away from the snowblower. What if that chip had hit your eye?" He shook his head and put on his gloves.

Lana put her arms around his waist. "I'm sorry, Grandpa," she whispered. He patted her arm and went out to finish removing the snow.

That's the way Lana was—quick to do something that got her in trouble, then quick to be sorry in order to get out of trouble.

The snow fell all day, and Grandma made us stay indoors after lunch. We didn't take naps anymore, so she made sure that we kept busy and quiet while Grandpa slept.

"What month is it?" she asked.

"I think it's November, because Mom was talking about getting a turkey," Lana said.

Grandma nodded. "That is what's printed on the calendar, but the Lakota call it 'Moon When Winter Sets In.' Why do you suppose that is?"

We both thought for a while. "I know," I said, "because that's when we get the first snow."

"That's not always so," Lana said. "Last year it snowed on Halloween."

"But most times it doesn't," I objected.

"Shh," Grandma cautioned as our voices grew loud.

We sat quietly before Lana asked, "Do the other months have Lakota names?"

"Yes," Grandma explained. "Before we had a calendar, the Indians named the time of the year after things that happened in nature."

She pulled a sheet of paper out of a drawer. "Here," she said, pointing to three columns on the page, "are the English names of the months, then the Lakota Moons written in Lakota, and what they mean in English."

She took the calendar off of the kitchen wall and turned the pages back to January. "I'll write the Lakota name on each month," she said. "Then you can copy them and the English meaning on next year's new calendar."

"Why did they call them 'moons'?" I asked.

"They knew the phases of the moon lasted for many days. It is sort of what is now known as a month."

She wrote, "January—Moon of the Terrible," and explained, "It was so named because of the terrible cold that caused many deaths.

"Then," Grandma went on, "the people had to spend most of the time in their tipis. Their breathing made the walls frosty. So, February was named Moon When There Is Frost inside the Lodge.

"March—Moon When the Frost Covers the Prairie Chickens' Eyes. The weather gets warm, then it gets cold again, and the poor prairie chickens wake up with frost on their eyelids.

"April—Moon When the Geese Return. The people were glad to have the geese come back because they were hungry after a long winter.

"May—Moon When the Leaves Turn Green.

"June—Moon When the Berries Are Ripe.

"July—Moon When the Choke Cherries Are Ripe.

"August—Moon When All Things Ripen.

"September—Moon When the Leaves Turn Yellow.

"October—Moon When the Leaves Blow Off.

"November—Moon When Winter Sets In. You already know this.

"December—Moon When Deer Shed Their Antlers.

"Now," Grandma continued as she handed each of us a new calendar, "you copy the names for next year. I'm going to rest for a bit. We'll bake cookies later—if you're quiet."

We wrote quietly until suddenly Lana shoved her chair back. "I'll finish later," she yawned. "Let's watch TV."

"I don't want to," I replied. "I want to copy the Moons so that I can show the calendar to Mom. You better do it now, or you won't ever do it."

"How do you know?" Lana asked.

"'Cause that's your usual lazy way."

"Well, I started. See," she said, handing me her calendar. In big letters on January's page she had printed MOON OF. Under the large words she'd written "terrible" in small letters. The rest of the months didn't have "moon of," only the descriptive words. She'd stopped at "leaves green."

"That's a lazy way," I smirked.

"I can't waste time writing 'moon of' twelve times. I think I'll draw pictures instead."

"It's not a waste of time—it's good practice to improve your handwriting."

"Oh, you think you're so smart," Lana yelled. "You always try to do everything better than me." She threw the calendar on the table.

"Shush," I said. "You'll wake them up, and then we'll be in trouble."

"And you'll tell them it's my fault!"

"It is!"

"Oh, be quiet!" she yelled.

"SHUSH!" I warned again.

"What's going on? I heard your yells in the bedroom!" Grandma said wearily.

"She's the one—" Lana sobbed and pointed at me.

"Hah!" I was glad to see her tears. I wouldn't cry. Lana always made me cry, but not this time!

"Time out!" Grandma ordered. "Lana, go to your room . . ."

"It's my room, too!" I said, taking a deep breath.

"You can have it!" Lana choked. "I don't ever want to be around you again!"

"That's fine with me!" I stormed.

"Lori, you go into the bedroom. Lana, you go to the kitchen."

I turned and stomped to the bedroom. My eyes burned, and I tried not to blink, because if I did, the tears would come. I wasn't going to cry! I was tired of Lana bossing me around and always having to have her way!

I remember staring wide-eyed out the window at the thickly falling snow. It was peaceful, unlike the way things were between Lana and me.

In the Lakota way Lana and I were not first cousins but sisters. This was because my mom, Marie, and Lana's mother, Martha, were sisters. I'm six months older than her, and the eldest child in a Lakota family is supposed to watch over and help care for younger children.

Doing things in the Lakota way was important to my family even though we didn't live in tipis. Grandpa believed that our values helped us get along as a family and with the rest of the world.

But sometimes I didn't follow the old way. I was older than Lana, but in no way did I watch over and care for her.

Lana was loud, adventurous, and willing to try anything. When she thought of something to play, we did it. She decided what cartoon show we'd watch or what story Grandpa should tell. When she got into trouble, I did too. I was the quiet, timid, and obedient child.

Grandma and Grandpa High Elk were our moms' parents, and we were a close family. We would have spent a lot of time with our grandparents even if none of our parents worked because that was also the Lakota way.

Grandma fixed up a room for Lana and me. Grandpa made a toy box and bookshelves for us. We had our own beds and a dresser drawer with clothes and pajamas for when we stayed over, like we had to this night. Our parents couldn't come for us because the streets were so clogged with heavy snow.

Darkness came early, and the snow still fell when Grandma called us to set the table. Grandma had kept us apart all afternoon. Now, I wasn't as angry as I had been.

After Grandpa said grace he told us, "Your food will not digest well when you're angry. So you both say 'sorry' before we eat."

I peeked at Lana, who was smiling at Grandpa. She walked around the table to my side. "Lori," she said softly, "I'm sorry."

I almost didn't respond. This was Lana's way—she knew she'd get out of trouble by apologizing. I blinked, stared over her shoulder, and saw Grandma nodding at me to say the words.

"Me too," I choked.

We were hungry and didn't talk much during supper. After we helped Grandma clear the table, we had baths. Then in our pajamas we sat by Grandpa's chair.

"Tell us about Iktomi," Lana asked.

"Oh, he's told us so many Iktomi stories, you've became an Iktomi," I said to Lana.

Iktomi was a character from Lakota stories. He tricked animals and people into doing things he wanted, but then he'd end up in trouble. Yet he never learned.

Lana looked puzzled and angry that I didn't want an Iktomi story. "What do you mean?" she asked.

"You do things that get you in trouble, and you get me in trouble, too."

Grandpa chuckled. "Lana does get herself and you in trouble, but I don't think she does it on purpose like Iktomi does."

"See," Lana smirked at me.

"You still get in trouble," I said.

"Whoa," Grandpa cautioned. He didn't like to hear us bickering. "You're both Iktomis—arguing about unimportant stuff. I think you'd better go to bed."

In the bedroom Grandma said, "Grandpa's tired from removing snow, and you are worn out from playing in it. Say your prayers."

We knelt by our beds. "Now I lay me down to sleep, I pray thee Lord my soul to keep. If I should die before I wake, I pray thee Lord my soul to take."

As I repeated the words, I felt a chill down my back.

"What's 'soul'?" I asked, "and where would the Lord take ours?"

"Our souls are what make us alive," Grandma explained. "The soul is the spirit in us that lives forever."

"Yeah," Lana said. "So the Lord will take our souls to heaven."

I shivered and wanted to ask where heaven was, but Grandma said, "You're cold. Get into bed." She tucked us in, kissed us, and turned out the lights. "Good night," she whispered as she shut the door.

I woke during the night to the wind howling around the corners of the house. I pulled the covers up, glad to be warm and safe in bed.

Grandma wouldn't let us out of the house the next morning. "It's too cold—maybe this afternoon. It's supposed to warm up. You don't go out either," she said to Grandpa.

"That darn wind drifted the snow over the driveway," he complained.

"We can't go anywhere until the street is plowed," Grandma said. "Tim will do it for you. There's no school today."

Grandpa was not supposed to do heavy work since his heart

attack, so he hired Tim the neighbor boy to help him. But sometimes Grandpa got impatient and did the work himself.

Lana wanted to watch TV, but I told her I was going to read. I was still miffed at her.

"Okay," she said. "Read me a story." I knew she was trying to make up.

"Read your own book," I said.

"I don't want to," she snapped.

"Well, I want to read to myself!"

"Girls," warned Grandma. So I read while Lana watched TV.

We didn't go outdoors until the afternoon. "Look," cried Lana, "our tracks are gone."

The wind had drifted snow over the driveway, covering our footsteps. There were also strange marks over our tracks.

Grandpa came to the backyard. "Now you girls stay back here while Tim runs the snowblower."

He looked at the tracks. "Hey, we have rabbits. See where they hopped under the bush? Probably looking for nibbles. Oh, I'll be! Here's deer. One or two jumped over the fence. Oh, oh, they've been eating on the shrubs."

We looked where he pointed. "All those animal tracks, and the wind covered the ones we made yesterday," I said.

"Yeah, Grandpa," Lana explained, "we made a circle, but it looked like just one person had walked in the snow."

He chuckled and then pointed at a spot by the garage. "There."

There were four footprints.

"They seem like they were made by one person, but look closer. See, here's Lana's boot, and Lori's inside it. You can tell that your feet are smaller than Lana's."

We saw what he meant.

"Can we put a box over them so they will last?" Lana wondered.

Grandpa smiled at us. "We can't keep snow from melting."

We must have looked sort of sad about that, so he added, "But they'll always be there."

"How can that be?" I asked. "When the snow melts we can't see them."

"I think the snow melts them in the ground. So even if we can't see them, they'll always be there."

"Oh, sure," I said, but I didn't believe him.

2. Moon When Deer Shed Their Antlers

The snow did melt, but soon we had more snow that covered the whole backyard.

We spent every day with Grandma and Grandpa. They had a lot of patience to care for Lana and me. When we were nine, they had another grandchild to watch. Lana got a brother.

"*Waste*!" Grandpa said when he heard the news. "It's about time we had a boy in this family! Maybe he'll want to go deer hunting."

"Grandpa," we groaned. He and our dads were hunters. We ate venison and other game that they brought home. Lana and I (for once we agreed) didn't want them to shoot deer. The deer were graceful and had beautiful eyes. We liked to see them in the yard. Grandma didn't like it when they ate the flowers and shrubs she'd planted. But Grandpa hated it when they got into his garden—he called them rats with antlers. He would love to have a boy he could teach to hunt.

Then he turned to Grandma. "I hope he won't be too much work for you?"

Grandma smiled and said, "It'll be good to have a baby in the house, and he'll be the only one. Not like having these two babies at the same time." She nodded at Lana and me. "The best part is that they're big enough to help take care of him."

"When is he going to be baptized?" Grandpa asked.

Our family attended St. Matthew's Episcopal Church, which followed many Lakota ways in worship and congregational activities. Grandma belonged to the Wiyan Ominiceye, a Lakota society of women who helped their people. This church group consisted mostly of grandmothers. They made quilts to raise money to send kids to church camp and to fund other things the congregation needed.

In the Lakota way, everybody had something to do that was helpful to the band. So our dads read the lessons, served as ushers, and did anything that Father Jim asked. Aunt Martha taught Sunday school. Grandpa used to mow lawns and shovel sidewalks until the doctor told him to stop. He got kind of grumpy when all he could do was go to services. So Father Jim talked him into being a lector and reading the first lesson.

When we got older I sang in the choir, and I was glad that Lana didn't because she sang like a frog. But then she became an acolyte—an assistant to Father Jim during services—and bragged, "It's too bad you're so little, this cross would probably be too heavy for you to carry."

"Oh, you always have to be better in everything!" I said.

"Oh? How about you? You were so braggy when you got into the choir and I didn't. Now I get to go first in the processions, and the choir will have to follow me!"

"We're not following you"—she made me so mad!—"we're following the cross!"

"But I'm carrying it!"

"Stop your bickering," Grandpa scolded. He didn't like to hear us argue.

We were all in church for the baby's baptism. He was christened Robert Edward and was named after Grandpa High Elk and Lana's grandpa Edward Dubray.

My mom and dad were his godparents and stood around the baptismal font with Aunt Martha and Uncle Joe. I had to stay in the choir but could see all that was going on. Lana, as an acolyte, was right there, too. She held the prayer book for Father Jim and handed him the stuff he needed.

It was a nice service. The baby didn't cry, but the rest of us got a little teary—even Lana, which surprised me.

I admit that I was jealous that Chuckie was Lana's brother. I didn't have any brothers or sisters. When I asked Mom and Dad why, they'd say, "You're the only one we want."

He was a cute baby. But we didn't call him Robert or Edward. "He's Chaske," Grandpa explained, "the firstborn son." So we called him Chuckie.

The firstborn daughter was supposed to be called Winona, but that didn't work for us—Lana and I couldn't both be Winona. I thought that I should be Winona since I really was the older daughter, but no one listened to me.

We played with Chuckie, "ooohed" and "ahhed" and "kootchied" at him, and we both wanted to hold him. Lana, as usual, got her way. She helped bathe and dress him and gave him his bottle. She'd hold him until he pooped, then she would give him to me.

He was really stinky, but even though I didn't know it then, changing diapers was practice for babysitting jobs when I was older. He was so sweet to cuddle after he was clean. I loved it when he wiggled and laughed after I poked his fat tummy.

But Lana got to play with Chuckie at home, and I only saw him at Grandma's after school. Then, when he turned three, Lana complained about him getting into her stuff. At Grandma's she ignored him, so I was the one he came to.

"Read . . . me . . . Lori," he begged, carrying an armload of books. I didn't mind reading to him; it was cozy sitting in Grandpa's chair with Chuckie snuggled in my lap. He was still sweet, even though he wasn't a baby any more.

Christmas vacation arrived—two whole weeks of no school. When the first snow came we took Chuckie to play in it. He followed Lana and me, stretching his legs to step where we did, so that it looked like only one person had walked there.

"But look," I showed him. "It looks like one print, but see, there's your foot, inside of mine, inside of the print of Big Foot—Lana's." He and I laughed but Lana didn't.

"It doesn't matter what size they are," Lana told him. "Tomorrow, they'll be gone—new snow will cover them or they'll melt. But Chuckie," she said very seriously, "our footprints will always be there, even if we can't see them anymore."

I remember Grandpa telling us that, but I wasn't sure it was true. Chuckie looked solemnly at the tracks and nodded, and I couldn't spoil the moment.

It was a busy time, even though there was no school. We had to get ready for Christmas at St. Matthew's.

The Saturday before Christmas all our family and others cleaned the church. The ladies had to make sure the church was spotless before the red poinsettias and green pine boughs were placed on the windowsills, the altar, and the organ. Everything had to be perfect for the Christmas Eve service.

Chuckie wanted to help, so Grandma gave him a rag to dust the pews. "You girls keep an eye on him," Grandma said.

We sort of forgot about him because his head was just barely above the pews. Then Lana said, "Oh, no," and she giggled as she pointed.

Chuckie had piled hymnals and prayer books in a high, crooked tower that leaned over the aisle. He stood on the pew and reached up to put another book on the top. He saw us watching, smiled, and poked a finger at the stack of books. He fell. The books clattered and thumped on the pew, the floor, and Chuckie. He started bawling, even though he wasn't hurt. He got a scolding, and we helped him put the books back in the pews.

"Lana, Lori," Aunt Martha asked, "please take Chuckie to play in the toy room downstairs."

She wanted him out of the cleaners' way, but she also didn't want him to see ladies filling brown paper bags with apples, oranges, peanuts, and hard candy. After the pageant each child would get one of these Christmas treats.

On Christmas Eve we got to church around five o'clock and helped the little ones into their costumes for the pageant. In the center before the altar was a toy crib filled with straw.

The church filled with parents and grandparents who came to watch the show. Joseph (who was really Andy Brown Wolf) walked with his head down and his face red as he shuffled to one side of the crib. Mary (who was Lana) followed with hands folded and a saintly smirk on her face.

Joseph and Mary knelt by the empty crib and held their hands like they were praying. But the towel on Joseph's head kept slipping over his eyes. Mary glared at him and whispered, loud enough for the congregation to hear, "Fix it!" And when he couldn't do it she gave an exasperated sigh, got up, and adjusted it for him. Then she returned to her place by the crib, and the saintly smirk returned.

An angel with crooked wings announced the birth of baby Jesus, and another angel showed up carrying a doll wrapped in a star quilt. The angel looked over the congregation for her parents, and somehow the baby slipped from its blanket. *Clunk* went its head on the crib rail. "Be careful," we heard Mary order. She rescued the doll and tenderly rewrapped it.

The shepherds came in the front door and strolled up the aisle to the altar. The sheep—Chuckie and other three- and four-year-olds—followed the shepherds. The crawled up the aisle in fuzzy sheep caps and shirts. "Baa, Baa, Baa," they all cried as they bumped into pews and the rear ends of each other. The Three Wise Men followed the sheep. They were older boys who looked bored with the whole event.

After the pageant we got our candy bags. Then we went to the basement for sandwiches and cake. After eating, most of the pageant actors went home with their grandmas.

But our family stayed for the late service. Lana lit the candles on the altar. Her mom and dad were ushers. Grandma and I were in the choir, while Mom played the organ.

Grandpa read the first lesson and then sat in a pew where Chuckie was asleep on the padded seat. My dad read the second lesson. The little church was crowded, and the flowers, greens, and candles made a lovely scene. Carrying the cross, Lana led the procession and was followed by the choir and Father Jim.

The congregation sang louder than the choir. "Amen's" resounded after the prayers. Then everyone sat and listened to Father Jim's sermon. I don't remember what he said because of what happened after he sat down.

It was time for the offering. Mom began playing the choir's anthem, and we stood as we sang, "What child is this?"

I thought our singing was wonderful. I saw Father Jim smile as he listened. Lana stood ready to take the offering plates from the ushers, while her mom and dad were at the rear of the church waiting for the song to end.

I saw Lana's shoulders stiffen. I couldn't see her face. Mom kept playing, but her lips tightened and her eyes kept glancing toward the aisle. I looked and saw Chuckie.

He was trying to get in the crib that had been set near the Christmas tree after the pageant. When he couldn't do that he started to dance while we sang. He held his arms straight out, bobbed his head in time to the music, and twirled around.

Those in the congregation who could see him were smiling, and others in the back were stretching their necks to see what was happening. The song ended. While his parents walked up the aisle with the plates, Chuckie bowed to the congregation. His dad grabbed his hand, and they walked to the altar.

We sang the Lakota doxology while Father Jim held the plates high toward the cross. Then he said, "Thank you for your offerings tonight, but thank you also for your gifts of your time and talents. This which is represented by this family"—meaning us. Then he gave the plates to a red-faced Lana to put away.

Dinner on Christmas Day was at my house. Aunt Martha and Mom took turns having holiday dinners and wouldn't let Grandma do anything but bring *wojape*. It is a pudding made from chokecherries, and Grandma used the cherries we had all picked last summer to make it. After the big meal we opened our presents.

I got books and a diary with a pen. Lana got videos and a sketchbook with colored pencils. We all, Chuckie too, got ice skates.

That afternoon our dads took us to the skating rink, which was glassy smooth. We put our skates on in the warming house. Uncle Joe helped Chuckie fasten his double-bladed skates to his shoes and then helped him onto the ice.

Dad glided smoothly over the ice to show me how to skate. I tried, but my ankles wobbled. I struggled to stay upright and carefully moved about the rink.

"Watch out!" Lana shouted as she ran onto the ice, jumped into the air, spun, and fell. "Whoops," she said breathlessly.

But she got up and did it again. She tried to jump and spin three times, and each time she fell. Then she quit. "That's it," she said and stumbled back to the warming house to take off her skates.

"Lana," Uncle Joe said, suppressing a grin, "what were you trying to do?"

"Skate," she replied in a gruff voice.

Then I knew. "She was trying to do fancy skating like on TV," I said.

She nodded. "The skaters on TV do it so easily, I thought I could, too."

"Lana, those skaters have been skating all of their lives—with hours of practice every day," Uncle Joe said.

But that was the end of skating for Lana. If she couldn't skate like a "pro" on her first try, she didn't want to do it at all.

3. Moon When There Is Frost inside the Lodge

The grown-ups laughed about Lana's skating attempt and urged her to keep trying, but she refused. The ice was getting sort of mushy as the days warmed, and it wasn't as much fun in the rink.

Lana spent hours indoors with her sketchbook. She drew a picture of Chuckie dancing in church, but this time with wings and a halo.

"He was so cute," Lana said. "Don't scold him," she urged her parents.

I didn't say it out loud, but I agreed with her. Chuckie was too sweet, precious, and little to be punished. But Grandpa High Elk said, "You girls are spoiling him. He's got to learn that he can't always do what he wants."

As winter continued Chuckie wouldn't be in the car when Grandpa picked us up after school. It was cold, and getting Chuckie in and out of his snowsuit and boots was a real chore for Grandma and Grandpa.

But back at the house, Grandpa made sure that Chuckie was busy doing something that didn't involve Lana and me. It was sort of boring without Chuckie to read to, and so was watching the TV cartoons that Lana liked to watch.

Lana and I argued a lot.

"I don't want to watch that dumb show. Turn it down so I can read," I complained.

Lana said, "Just because your nose is always in a book, doesn't mean mine should be!"

I responded, "You watch TV 'cause you can't read!"

By then, we were shouting at each other. Grandma ordered, "STOP!!"

She'd send one of us to our room or to help with Chuckie and the other outside if it were warm.

Then one evening when both of our moms came for us, Grandma made an announcement.

"Grandpa and I have decided it's time for the girls to have new names."

"Why?" Lana asked. "What's wrong with the ones we already have?"

"They're good names, but I'm talking about Lakota names," Grandma said. "We want you to know about the customs of the tribe, and part of that is to give you a Lakota name.

"Lori," she said to me. "Grandpa will give you 'Pejuta Okawin.' That was his mother's name."

"Peh-ju-tah oak-ah-whin," I repeated. "What does it mean?"

"'All-Around Medicine Woman.' She was called that because she was a highly respected healer. She knew how to use plants and herbs for medicine."

"Will I have to know about that stuff, too?"

"Only if you want to," Grandma said.

She turned to Lana. "I'll give you the name of my grandmother, 'Skanskanwin,' which means 'Moving Woman.' She was called that because when it was time for her camp to move, she was the one who made sure that all was packed and ready to go."

"Ska-ska-whin," Lana said. "That's a good name for me, too. I like to go places. But what do I do with 'Lana'?"

Grandma laughed. "You'll both keep the names you have. The new ones are special family names, like the Lakota used to have.

"In those days before our people had to live on reservations," Grandma told us, "a newborn baby was given a name like 'Red Leaf' if it were born in the autumn, when the leaves turned color. Or a name like 'Morning Star' might be given because the baby was born when the morning star appeared."

"I like those names," I said. "Was I born in the morning?"

"No," Mom said. "It was two o'clock in the afternoon."

"I was born in winter, so what kind of name would I have?" Lana asked.

"You'd be 'Snowball,'" I giggled.

Aunt Martha smiled. "She'd be 'Stormy' because there was a blizzard."

Grandma went on, "When a child was ten to twelve years old, the baby name was often changed. Children would be honored in a special ceremony and given a new name. When this was done, all the people knew that this child was very much loved by her family."

Lana and I looked at each other. We understood what our grandparents were doing for us.

"We want to have the naming before school starts in the fall. You will have to help us prepare for the ceremony. There's going to be a lot to do, and we only have a few months to get ready."

She asked Mom and Aunt Martha, "Can you go shopping this weekend? I want to show the girls how to make a star quilt, and we'll need fabric."

So on Saturday Mom, Aunt Martha, Grandma, Lana, and I went to the fabric shop at the mall. Grandma led us to the quilting section, but there were so many different patterns and colors that it was impossible to choose between them.

Of course, Lana wouldn't agree with the color I wanted—she chose green. I wanted red.

"If," Grandma said, "we use green and red, it'll be a Christmas quilt. How about if we choose traditional colors," she murmured as she picked varying shades of reds and yellows. "Now some black, and we'll use white for the background."

So, on our first after-school evening with Grandma, she began to teach us how to quilt.

"The first thing we do," Grandma explained, "is launder and

dry the material. This ensures that the colors are set, so that they don't bleed into each other in the quilt. We also wash out the sizing or finish on the fabric so that it will be soft and easy to quilt."

I carefully followed directions, and I enjoyed the next step, when we ironed the wrinkles out of the dried fabric. We took turns doing this, but Lana complained, "Why do we have to iron out the wrinkles? Such a boring thing to do."

Grandma had made many star quilts in her lifetime and needed no pattern to follow. Her design was the traditional "Morning Star"— one large, five-pointed star made from different-colored diamond pieces that were sewn together.

"Are your hands clean?" Grandma asked us every day after school.

Lana complained, "Why do we always have to wash—we wash at school, then we wash at home—I'm not going to have any hands left, I wash them so much!"

"What did you have for lunch?" Grandma asked. When we said "pizza," she continued, "And you ate it with your fingers, right?" We nodded. "So that grease from the pizza is still on your fingers even if you washed you hands after lunch. Those grease marks might not show on the quilt while we're working on it, but years later that grease will darken—it'll be ugly."

We washed our hands.

"Today we'll cut diamonds," Grandma said. She gave each of us a stiff piece of paper. "This is a template, a pattern. Trace around it with chalk on the cloth.

"Now, cut." She gave us scissors. "Be careful because they are sharp. Take care to follow the lines."

"This takes so long," Lana complained. "Why don't we put four layers together and then cut?"

Grandma explained that the diamonds all had to cut in the same direction, or they would not fit when we got to sewing. "Otherwise, the quilt would have a crooked star. Some quilters don't care how they cut or sew," Grandma scornfully said. "They're in too much of a hurry. But when the quilt is done," she laughed, "if there's a tipi in the middle"—she poked up the center into a cone shape—"it'll never lay flat."

When our mothers came after us, I was glad to stop. My fingers were tired from using the scissors.

"Oh, let me help," Aunt Martha said. "I used to like to cut diamonds."

"I'd rather sew them together," said my mom.

They recalled how Grandma had taught them to quilt when they were the same age as Lana and me.

"Oh, don't you wish we had time to do this," sighed Aunt Martha to my mom.

"You can help with the quilting," Grandma said. "That takes the most time."

While we were in school Grandma cut more diamonds "so that we can get to the sewing," she said. "Even with three of us cutting, it takes a long time to get all of the diamonds done."

"Grandma," I asked, "why do you always make star quilts?"

"When the Lakota had to move to reservations," she explained as she worked, "white ladies came to teach them new ways. The Indian women learned to use a steel needle instead of a bone awl.

"They no longer had buckskin to make clothes, so they learned to sew cloth in shirts and dresses. There were always scraps of cloth left over, so they learned to make quilts from the pieces. They made crazy quilts. They made patch quilts. But their favorite was the star quilt."

"Why?" asked Lana.

"It reminded them of the Morning Star that rises in the east and begins a new day. They believed the Morning Star also stood for a new life. So the women made the Morning Star in their quilts as they began a new life on reservations."

Lana sat quietly watching and listening to Grandma. Being quiet wasn't normal for her—she usually wiggled, poked herself, and didn't do much quilting. Well, she still wasn't doing much quilting—she was too busy listening.

Time seemed to go fast when we were at Grandma's; soon we had all of the pieces sewn together. Grandma now showed us how to layer the quilt. First came the back, then the fluffy batting, and finally the quilt top.

Next she showed us how to make even stitches in the quilt.

"Ouch." Lana had poked her finger. Grandma gave us each a thimble.

Before we went home, we threaded needles for Grandma, because she had trouble seeing the tiny eye. Once a week Grandma's friends from the Wiyan Ominiciye came to help her quilt.

They'd often be there when we got to Grandma's after school. We liked to listen to the ladies talk as we all quilted.

"Mrs. Blue Shield had an honoring for her son who came back from the war. We helped her make twenty quilts for the giveaway."

"Next year I will give my grandson a name."

"You've helped me, so I will help you make the quilts for his naming ceremony," promised Grandma.

"Why do you give the quilts away?" I wanted to know.

"Quilts are given to show thanksgiving for special events in a person's life. It's sort of like a reverse birthday party. The one

who is having the birthday gives gifts instead of the guests bringing presents.

"Quilts are given to show thanks for so many things, like a
new baby, graduation from high school and college, or the safe
return of warriors. They can be made to celebrate weddings or
any special event, like your naming. Sometimes a quilt covers
a casket at a funeral."

I tried to make smaller and more even stitches. I realized
that this quilt was a special thing and that it was an honor to
work on it.

4. Moon When the Geese Return

We worked on the quilt after school, and the winter passed quickly to the windy, chill days of March. It was cozy in the warm house. As we quilted we talked about our day at school.

I was a grade ahead of Lana, but we could have been in the same grade. Our mothers had talked about holding me back so that Lana and I would have started together. But my dad said no.

"Lori's five years and four months old when school starts," he noted. "She knows her numbers, she can write her name and telephone number, and she can even read a little bit." Later he told me that he thought that Lana and I should learn how to get along with children besides each other.

On my first day of school, Lana cried, "I want to go too."

I was scared but excited as I got into Grandpa's car. It was strange to be without Lana, but I didn't miss her. Every day she rode with grandpa to pick me up at school, and she usually asked, "What did you do in school today, Lori?"

She liked to be read to, and I tried to teach her the words the way Mrs. Arnold did in school. Lana would repeat them, and I thought she could read. But when she started school she didn't like reading.

One of the exciting times at school was when High Eagle, a Lakota hoop dancer, visited. All the classes met in the gym and watched him lay out the hoops all around him. At the same time he told us about the values of the old ways.

"These hoops represent sharing, bravery, and honesty." He held up a hoop for each value. "They come from the Lakota heritage but are important to all people.

"This hoop"—he lifted the fourth high above his head—"is wisdom. This is most important to you right now in school, where you must learn so that you will become wise adults." He nodded to his assistant, who turned on the cassette player, and drumbeats boomed through the gym.

Then High Eagle started spinning the hoops on his arms and legs. With one foot he flipped a red hoop up over an arm. "This is for the Red People—we Indians."

He moved in time to the drum music, keeping all of the hoops spinning, and flipped more hoops onto his arms. "The Black, the Yellow, and the White," he said.

The hoops spun faster and moved from his arms to his legs and head. He flipped up a rainbow-colored hoop and explained, "And this is for the people who are a mixture."

Now all the hoops were joined together into one intricate form, and he moved so fast we couldn't tell one color from another.

Finally the beats slowed, the hoops fell away, and he stood alone in the center of the gym. The kids cheered and clapped as he bowed to each part of the room.

"*Pilamiye*—thank you," he said, and held his hands up for silence. "Are there any American Indians in this room?"

I raised my hand and looked around. There were a lot of hands up. Lana was waving hers so high and wildly that Mr. High Eagle called on her.

"I'm Indian!" she proudly claimed.

"Good," he said. "What tribe?"

"Lakota," Lana said proudly.

The elder nodded to Andy Brown Wolf, who was sitting next to Lana. "You?" he asked.

"I'm Cheyenne," Andy said.

"You're not either," said a white boy sitting next to Andy.

"Am too," he replied.

The other boy stared, smiled, then poked his buddy and whispered, "Okay, if you're an Indian, we get to put you in the cupboard!"

Many nearby kids laughed, and Lana glared at the boys, but Mr. High Eagle continued: "I'm glad that there are so many Indian students in school. You need to keep going all the way through high school and more." He waved his arms to include the whole gym. "You all need to do the best you can in school."

He began placing hoops around the gym floor. "Now," he said, "you will all get a chance to dance with the hoops. I only have enough for twenty at a time, so you'll have to take turns. That's part of the sharing value."

The teachers divided the students so that all of us got a chance to dance with the hoops. When it was my turn, I found that I could spin one around my waist easily, like a hula hoop, but when I tried to keep it going and spin two on my arms I couldn't do it.

But Lana and Andy Brown Wolf twirled with three hoops, and the rest of us stopped to watch. Mr. High Eagle encouraged them, remarking, "Good! Now try one on your leg."

Both managed to flip one up, but Andy stumbled and fell. Lana twirled the hoop on her leg for a minute before she lost her balance and all of the hoops clattered to the floor.

All the kids clapped and cheered except me. Lana was such a show off.

Mr. High Eagle said, "You all did a good job. You tried the best that you could to do a difficult thing—that's what you should always do." He bowed and said again, *"Pilamiye."*

After the assembly we were so excited that it was hard to get back to our lessons, so the teachers let us out for recess.

The two boys who had teased Andy about going in the cupboard were waiting for him. They boasted, "Come on, let's get him! We'll put him in the dumpster—it's like a cupboard."

They were bigger than Andy, and though he struggled, they dragged him over the playground. Suddenly Lana was there.

"Let him go!" she yelled with clenched fists.

"Get outta the way!" One boy shoved her.

Quickly Lana slammed her elbow into his nose and kicked the other in the leg. Andy fell to the ground.

Both tormenters hollered, and one grabbed Lana's arm. Andy jumped up and pulled Lana's other arm. "Let her go!"

The struggling group was surrounded by kids yelling, "Fight! Fight!" and teachers ran to stop the battle.

Lana, Andy, and the two other boys had to go to the principal's office. Later I asked Lana what happened.

"Mr. Parker scolded us and said we should respect each other and that one didn't put real people in the cupboard and certainly not in a dumpster.

"He made us say 'sorry.'" Lana grabbed my arm, "Now don't tell Grandma or my folks. I promised I wouldn't get into any trouble this week."

I didn't tell on her, but Andy's mother did. Lana was scolded for fighting, but she wasn't punished. They were all proud of Lana for standing up to those bullies. I was too, but I didn't tell her.

Most of the days at school were calm, however, like they were at the High Elk house.

From the time we first stood by ourselves, Grandma had marked our heights on the doorway of our room. My marks were in blue, and Lana's were in red. They were the same height until suddenly Lana's was an inch higher and the next year three inches higher. Not only was Lana taller than me, but her whole body and feet grew bigger.

Aunt Martha gave my mom the clothes that were too small for Lana. I hated them. Lana spilled or dribbled what she ate or drank, and all her T-shirts had grayish stains that Aunt Martha couldn't get out. I'd try not to wear one of her discards to school because if Lana recognized a shirt, she'd say, "Ooh, there's my favorite shirt. I wished I could still wear it, but I'm so much bigger." So all the kids knew it was a hand-me-down.

I hated being embarrassed and was glad that we weren't in the same class.

In the spring a new girl came to our school. She said she was Laotian-Hmong, and her name was Shoua Vang. She was as tall as me, and our skin color was about the same. Her hair was short and black, and her beautiful dark eyes were like those of a shy deer.

Before Shoua came to our school she had been in the ESL classroom. That is where kids from foreign countries learn English before they come to regular school.

Mrs. Arnold seated Shoua in the desk next to mine and asked me, "Lori, will you be a class mentor for Shoua and help her with her English?"

I proudly agreed because only smart kids were asked to be mentors.

Shoua didn't need any help with reading, but sometimes she'd say words in an odd way and the other kids would laugh. That's when I helped her. She was shy and quiet, but we got to be best friends.

No matter how cold and windy it was, Shoua was at school waiting by the front door for me. After school she waited until Grandpa came. Then she'd wave and walk home.

One evening Grandpa saw that she was shivering in her light jacket and didn't have a cap or gloves. "Get in Shoua; we'll give you a ride. You'll freeze before you get home."

She climbed in, "Thank you, Mr. High Bear." she said quietly.

"You can call him 'Grandpa,'" Lana said. "All of our friends do."

I didn't like that. *Our* friends? Shoua was my friend!

"That'll be fine," Grandpa said. "Do you have a grandfather in Laos?"

"No," Shoua whispered. "My grandpa and grandma both died in the camp before we came to the United States."

"I'm sorry," Grandpa said.

After that Shoua rode with us every day.

Later Grandpa told us what he had found about the Vang family. During the Vietnam War many Hmong people had fought the Communists in Laos. After the war they had to leave Laos or be killed. The Vang clan traveled at night through the jungle to a camp in Thailand. They had very little food. Shoua's baby brother died on the way, and Shoua was very sick when they reached the camp. They lived at the camp for many years until they were allowed to come to the United States.

The Vangs had hoped to go to Minneapolis, where many of their kinfolk had been moved. But the government thought that they would become Americans more quickly if they were separated from the others. They would have to learn English and get used to American ways.

Grandpa found out that the Vangs learned some English in the camp in Thailand, and Mr. Vang quickly found a job at the packing plant. Mrs. Vang had trouble with the language and stayed alone until Shoua got home. Then they would walk to the convenience store to buy food for supper.

"That's no place to buy groceries," Grandma said. "The prices are too high."

So Grandma and Grandpa took Shoua and her mother to the supermarket. Then Grandma told Mom and Aunt Martha about Mrs. Vang, and they began helping her with her English.

Aunt Martha quit giving me Lana's clothes and gave them to Mrs. Vang for Shoua. "I hope you don't mind," Aunt Martha said to me.

"Oh, no," I replied. "I'm glad Shoua can wear them."

I worried that Lana would gloat over Shoua wearing hand-me-downs, but to my surprise she didn't.

5. Moon When the Leaves Turn Green

It was spring, and we didn't want to sit in the house after school to work on the quilt—that is, until Grandma invited Mrs. Vang and Shoua to join us. Shoua was so excited to be there that Lana and I didn't mind staying indoors. Shoua was also curious about the colors in the quilt.

Grandma took a few stitches and explained.

"We—the Lakota—believe that the four directions each have a special color that represents some part of life."

Grandma spoke slowly so that Mrs. Vang could follow what she was saying, or she'd pause while Shoua translated the English for her mother.

"Yellow is the color of East—like the colors of a sunrise of a new day. The East represents birth and children who are just beginning to learn to live in the circle. Spring is the season of the East.

"Red is the color of South. It symbolizes the warmth of summer. This direction also stands for midday, noontime, and for adults who are in the prime of their life in the circle.

"White is the color of North. It is the color of snow and the hair of old people. The season of the North is winter. North also stands for the hardships that elders endured. In their long lives they have gained courage, strength, and wisdom. North signifies evening, the ending of a day, and also the closing years of life.

"Black is the color of West. It is the dark of the night after the sun sets. Autumn is its season—the time when the leaves on the trees and other plants die and when people die of old age."

After Grandma quit talking, we all sat quietly thinking of what she said. Later, in my room, I wrote a poem in my diary to help me remember the special colors of the four directions.

Yellow is the East,
The season of spring.
Golden rays of the rising sun

Bring light and life
To a new day.

Red is the South,
Warm summer,
The growing time
When life is good
In the noon of day.

Black is the West
The season of autumn's
Falling leaves
And spirits follow
The setting sun.

White is the North
Snow, the hardships of
Long life give strength.
It is the color
Of wise Grandma's hair.

I let Shoua read it.

"Oh," she said. "That's nice. My mom said that we had special colors, too. Some of our people were called green or blue because some had been dark or evil. Others are white, which has a safer meaning."

"Why don't you write a poem about them?" I asked.

She shook her head. "I don't know that much to write about. My mom says she wished her parents had told her more. But they were always moving to stay alive. We're very glad to be in the United States and not worry about war."

"I'm glad you're here, too." I said.

"What are you guys doing?" Lana came into the room. She hated to be left out.

"Oh, nothing," I said and shut my diary. I wouldn't show the poem to her. I knew she'd make fun of it.

After school Andy Brown Wolf started hanging out with us while we waited for Grandpa. Up until then most boys we knew were rough and liked to push and shove us around, but not Andy. Shoua and I teased, "Lana's got a boyfriend." We expected an angry denial, but Lana replied quietly, "Yeah, guess so. Andy is my boyfriend."

Sometimes he and Lana would talk about someone or something in their grade. He taught her how to play hacky sack, and she thought she was so smart that she could do it and we couldn't.

Then Lana said, "Andy plays on the boys' soccer team. I'm going to try out for the girls' team."

I didn't know what to say to that.

"My father played soccer at the camp," Shoua recalled. "We used to watch the games."

"Why don't you try out?" Lana asked.

"I don't know—I'll have to ask my father."

"Ask him, it'll be fun," Lana said.

"Will you try out?" Shoua asked me. Before I could answer Lana responded, "Oh, Lori's not athletic. She's a bookworm."

"What's a bookworm?" Shoua asked.

"That means I love to read," I said, miffed at Lana. "I used to read to Lana."

"I'm a bookworm, too," Shoua said.

"Well, ask your dad," Lana said.

The next day Shoua told me, "Dad said no, because I would need shoes and a uniform, and we don't have the money. Maybe next year—we'll start saving."

I felt sorry for Shoua, even though I really didn't want her to play soccer with Lana.

At lunch she told the news to Lana, who said, "That's too bad."

In the period after lunch, Mrs. Arnold went to see who was knocking on the classroom door. It was Lana with a note. The teacher read it and then called Shoua and me. "You may go with Lana to the counselor's office," she announced.

"Uh, oh," I thought, now what's Lana gotten us into? "What's up?" I asked her.

"I went to see Mr. Richardson right after lunch," she explained. "I told him that you, me, and Shoua had some problems to discuss and asked him if would he help us."

Mr. Richardson was the counselor who came to our school twice a week. He had given Lana passes for the three of us to go to his office.

"What problems?" Shoua asked.

"Wait," Lana stated, and we followed her into the counselor's office.

"Hi, Lori, Shoua," he greeted. "Come in." We sat at the round table in his office. "Lana said you three had something you wanted to talk about."

"Mr. Richardson," Lana began. "You know that Lori and me are American Indians?"

He nodded.

"Indian kids get school stuff from Mr. Johnson O'Malley, right?"

"Well, yes. But Johnson-O'Malley is not a person. The name refers to two different men—U.S. Congressmen whose last names were given to a special law."

"Oh," acknowledged Lana.

"That law allows the school district to get money from the government for Indian students in special circumstances."

"Indian kids can get supplies and things like uniforms and gym shoes, right?"

Now I knew Lana's plan. She was going to try to get soccer equipment for Shoua.

"Okay. We want to get Shoua in the program. She looks like us." Lana motioned to us to stand up. We stood side-by-side in front of a mirror.

She was right. Our skin color was about the same. Shoua's hair was blacker than ours, her eyes were shaped a bit differently, and Lana was taller than her. But all three of us did look much alike.

"Shoua could be an Indian," Lana announced.

"Oh," Shoua smiled, "could I?"

"Yeah," I nodded in agreement. Lana had a good idea—for a change.

Mr. Richardson put his hand over his mouth, and his eyes twinkled like he wanted to laugh, but he didn't.

"That's a good thought you girls have, but there are . . . rules. Shoua has to prove that she has Indian blood."

That stopped Lana, who frowned and looked at me.

"I read a story once," I announced, concentrating to remember it. "It was about an Indian boy from a long time ago in the colonies. His tribe had found this orphan white boy. They became good friends, then soldiers came to take the white boy back. The tribe was going to let them, but the boys ran away and then became blood brothers—so the tribe kept him."

"Oh, good idea!" Lana said. "If boys could be blood brothers, why can't girls be blood sisters?"

"How do we do that?" Shoua asked.

"In the story they cut their arms and let their blood run together," I remembered.

"Wait a minute," Mr. Richardson said. "Even if you had trans-fusions, that wouldn't make Shoua an Indian."

"But you said she had to have Indian blood," Lana reminded him.

"Yeah, if we did it here in your office, you could say that she had Indian blood to prove it," I reasoned.

He shook his head, his hand over his mouth again. "I'm sorry, girls. I'm afraid it won't work. The government has strict rules."

We argued some more, but it didn't do any good.

When we got up to leave, Mr. Richardson said to Shoua, "Even though you can't be made an Indian, you're lucky to have two good friends."

"I know," she said shyly and squeezed our hands.

6. Moon When the Berries Are Ripe

Spring came, but neither Lana nor Shoua played soccer. Lana's grades were bad, and if she didn't improve them, she'd have to go to summer school.

"Can Lori help Lana with her homework?" Aunt Martha asked. "We can't seem to get her to do it—she says she doesn't have time."

Of course Mom said yes, and I had to help Lana, even though I didn't want to.

I was sitting reluctantly at the dining room table and looking at Lana's reading assignment when the doorbell chimed.

It was Andy. He was going to help Lana. I was glad I didn't have to do it but was miffed that she worked so willingly with him when she'd argue with me.

Lana passed every class, so when school was over, she, Chuckie, and I stayed all day with Grandma and Grandpa and helped with their garden.

When our moms were little girls, Grandma and Grandpa ranched on the reservation. Then Grandpa had a heart attack and almost died. I was little, but I remember how worried Mom was that we'd lose Grandpa.

But he got better. "I guess the ancestors didn't want me yet," he said. Still, he had to give up the ranch because he could no longer work so hard, so he didn't complain about moving to town. He was pleased when they found a home that almost seemed like it was in the country. It was located in a pretty spot in the valley that bordered a small stream and had rich black dirt for Grandpa's garden.

Grandma helped with the garden but complained that they didn't need such a big one. Grandpa, however, reasoned that gardening was the only work the doctor approved for him and that our moms enjoyed fresh vegetables. Lana and I toddled after them as soon as we walked and enjoyed playing in the dirt—until

Lana ate some, and we had to stay out. But soon we were helping tend to the plants.

Grandpa gave each of us a whole row in the garden to take
care of. He showed us how to sow tiny seeds in even lines, tamp
the soil evenly over them, and gently water so as not to wash
the seeds out of their row. I was thrilled when tiny green shoots
sprouted from the black dirt. Next we learned how to thin the
plants so that the strongest would have room to grow. We weed-
ed and watered so that at the end of the summer we harvested
beans and peas or pulled carrots and turnips.

I did this all very carefully, the way Grandpa showed us, but
as usual Lana hurried. The plants in her row meandered crook-
edly; peas mixed with carrots. There were big gaps between
plants because she jerked the weeds instead of pulling them, in
the process loosening the good plants, too.

"Don't be in such a hurry," Grandma would chide her, but
Lana had no patience. "It takes so long to do all that," she fussed,
bored with gardening.

After Chuckie was old enough not to eat dirt, we took him with
us into the garden, and Lana showed him how to pull weeds.

"See, Chuckie, you take your two fingers and lift it out. Oh,
what a big boy you are. You can pull weeds all by yourself!" Of
course I knew that was her way of getting out of the weed-pull-
ing chore.

After Shoua became our friend, she would often spend days
with us in the valley. "Since it's too late to plant," Lana said, "you
can have my garden row."

"Oh, thank you," Shoua proclaimed, thrilled. "I've never had
a garden. My mother talks about growing rice and vegetables
in Laos, but I don't remember that."

Then she asked Grandma, "Can my mother come to the garden, too?"

Mrs. Vang was excited to see the garden. She struggled with English, but Grandma understood how happy she was to have her hands in the soil. Grandma let her break up a larger area for her own plants. She was disappointed to learn that rice couldn't grow here but happily helped sow corn.

She showed Shoua how to reseed the bare spots in the row Lana gave her. When tiny sprouts appeared, she crawled carefully between the rows to gently thin the plants so that the strongest would grow. No weed dared to grow amongst her plants.

"I'll take care of the watermelons," Lana offered. "They need lots of water, and besides, the vine doesn't have to grow in a straight line."

That was okay with me. Sometimes there were snakes under the sprawling prickly vines. Every day Lana reported on the growth of the melons.

"They're getting this big," she said, making a circle of her arms.

"How do you know when they're finished growing?" I asked.

"You thump 'em." Lana demonstrated by thumping Chuckie. "When they sound like your head—hollow—they're ripe."

"Ow!" he complained. "My head isn't hollow. Yours is!" And he thumped her back.

Soon we were all thumping each other, until Chuckie started to cry.

"Here now," Grandpa said. "You girls get too rough. Come on, Chuckie, it's time for our naps."

Grandma and Grandpa rested in the afternoon. He would doze in the shade of the front porch; she went to her bed next to Chuckie's cot. We girls didn't have to lie down but were cautioned to stay out of trouble.

While Shoua and I read, Lana would get her sketchbooks and

draw green horses, purple bears, and blue cats. We stayed quiet until Lana got bored.

"Shh," Lana whispered and motioned to us to follow her to the garden.

In the melon patch she pointed to a melon and said, "This one's ripe." The thump she gave the watermelon did make it sound hollow. I helped her lift it and break it from the vine. We rolled the melon into the corn patch, out of sight of the house. We lifted it as high as we could and dropped it. It bounced but didn't break. Twice more we tried dropping it, until Lana found a rock to crack it open. This time the melon burst.

Warm, sweet, delicious! We gorged ourselves until we heard, "LAN-AH, LOR-REE! SHO-AH!" It was Grandma calling us.

Uh, oh. We wiped sticky fingers on our clothes and swatted away flies.

"Where have you been?" Grandma asked as we neared the porch.

"Come here!" she commanded. She took our faces in her hands, turned them from side to side and said, "You've been eating watermelon!"

We looked at each other. How did she know? Now I realize that our faces were sticky and smeared with dirt and that we looked guilty.

Grandma gave a big sigh, as if she really felt bad at our naughtiness. "Did you eat it all?"

We shook our heads no.

Grandpa got up from his chair. "Let's go get it," he said.

About half of the melon was still in one piece, so Grandpa took it to the kitchen. We picked up dirt-covered chunks and took them to the compost pile. Now the flies really buzzed around the sticky, dried juice on our faces and arms.

As our punishment we had no afternoon snack, and we had
to sit and watch Grandma, Grandpa, and Chuckie relish chilled
watermelon.

"You know girls," Grandpa said, "I was going to pick this melon tomorrow, but you beat me to it. If I had known you were so
anxious to eat it, I would have picked it earlier. It's better to ask
for what you want rather than stealing it."

"I'm sorry," Lana whispered.

"Me too," Shoua and I said.

Grandma and Grandpa smiled at us, but they still didn't give
us any melon.

For a few weeks we had to stay in the house during rest-time.
Lana quietly kept busy with her sketching while I read.

Once when Shoua was at the house Lana drew our faces. The
drawings did look like us, but Shoua's nose was crooked, and
my ears stuck out.

One day Lana couldn't be still any longer.

"Shoua," she whispered, "do you know what's in the attic?"

"No," Shoua answered. "I don't know what an attic is."

"It's the space between the ceiling and the roof of the house,"
I told her.

"Yeah," Lana agreed, "and there's a *chichi* in it."

"Oh, there isn't either," I corrected. "That's what Grandpa
used to tell us when we were Chuckie's age to keep us from
going to attic."

"What's a *chichi*?" Shoua asked.

"Come on," Lana said, "I'll show you."

"Lana, you're going to get in trouble again," I warned her.

"Not unless you tell," she retorted. "Come on, Shoua, there's
all kinds of neat things in the attic, like old bows and arrows
that Indians used to hunt buffalo."

"Really?" said Shoua curiously. She followed Lana, while I stayed on the couch with my book. I heard them slowly open the door to the stairs. It squeaked a little. Then it was quiet for a long time. Now I was curious. How could they get up the steps without making any noise? I got up, saw the door open, and peered up into the dusty gloom.

"Lana," I tried to call quietly and moved up the stairs.

"*CHICHI*!" A voice croaked from the attic. Then Shoua screamed and bumped into me. I grabbed the rail to keep from tumbling down, but Shoua fell.

From above Lana was saying, "Shh, shh, it's all right. Shh!"

"What's going on?" It was Grandpa.

I helped Shoua up, and she was holding her head. "Ow," she moaned.

We were in trouble again. Shoua had a bump that turned a swollen black and blue even after Grandma put ice on it.

"What happened, Lori?" Grandma asked. But I only shook my head. I wasn't going to tell.

"Lana?" Grandma asked.

"I just wanted to play a joke," Lana mumbled. "We went to the attic—Shoua wanted to see arrows and stuff. But it was dark and dusty, and I couldn't find them. I decided that we should come back down. I saw that old thing that looks like your body—you know—what you used to put your dress on?"

Grandma nodded.

"I shoved it at Shoua and said *chichi*. I didn't mean for her to get hurt." She looked at the floor, and there were tears on her cheeks. "I'm sorry."

Shoua wasn't badly injured, and soon the bruise faded. Lana, who had known that the attic was off-limits, wasn't allowed to watch TV for a week. Because I hadn't kept Lana from going to the attic, I couldn't watch TV either (which I didn't mind, but Grandma didn't know). But Mr. and Mrs. Vang kept Shoua home for a week.

When her parents brought her back, Mrs. Vang asked, "What is this *chichi?*"

"It's an imaginary thing that we use to keep children away from places that might get them in trouble," Grandpa started to explain.

Grandma went on, "When my grandmother was a little girl, her family lived in tipis and hunted buffalo, often in enemy territory. Other times the army was chasing them. Children had to be quiet in dangerous times so that their crying or noise would not give the tribe away.

"So soon after a baby was born, the mother began training the child to be quiet. When the baby cried, she put her hand over its nose and mouth and whispered *chichi*. It stopped, because it couldn't catch its breath. After doing this many, many times, all the mother had to do was touch the baby's face and it would stop. Then when the child was walking and the mother couldn't touch it's face to make it be still, all she had to say was *chichi*, and the child knew there was danger near and that he or she must not make any noise."

"Oh," said Mr. Vang, "so it is not an evil spirit. We worried that some evil being had come to harm the girls."

"No," Grandpa chuckled, "nothing bad. Just a bit of mischief."

But Shoua didn't come over so often after that. Lana and I didn't spend much time together either. I began going down by the creek during the afternoons.

The little creek along the garden is never very deep, and in the summer it flows in a narrow trickle. When the water is low,

Grandpa lets us play in it. We made mud pies or little dams and enjoyed the coolness of the shaded stream. But if it looked like rain, we had to hustle back to the house. The tiny trickle could quickly turn into a rushing flood.

Now we were allowed to play at the creek by ourselves. I liked to take an old foam cooler with sodas and snacks for the afternoon and lay on the bank with my book. Lana followed me, but I ignored her as she sat in the streambed and dug holes to watch them fill up with water.

One day the sky clouded over, and big wet plops hit my book. I picked up my book and started back to the house. "Come on, Lana," I called.

The rain came harder, and by the time we got to the house we were soaked.

It rained all afternoon, and the water spread over the creek bank. The next day was sunny, and most of the water had receded, but the creek was deeper than usual, and we waded knee-high in the muddy stream.

"I wish we had a boat," I said.

"Yeah," agreed Lana. Then she stopped, looked at the cooler, and got a funny gleam in her eye, which signaled that she had a new idea.

She dumped the ice and soda from the cooler and put it in the creek. The cooler bobbed down the stream.

"Hold it," she said to me, and I steadied it as she climbed in. It was a tight fit with her knees drawn up to her chin. The cooler sank lower in the stream, but it wobbled, turned, and floated. Lana began paddling with her hands to make it go faster.

I followed along the bank and laughed as the cooler picked up speed and Lana grabbed hold of the sides. Suddenly she broke through the bottom of the cooler, and water rushed up into it.

"Lori!" she screamed.

I waded into the creek, caught the cooler, and jerked it apart. Lana was trying to keep her face out of the water, and she grabbed at my arm and I fell. We both floundered about trying to get to our feet as the broken parts of the cooler floated away.

We finally crawled, splashed, and stumbled to our feet and waded out of the creek.

"Now what?" It was Grandpa coming down to the creek. "Are you two okay?"

We nodded. Our parents had told us not to get Grandpa upset—his heart didn't need a lot of excitement.

"We're okay, Grandpa," we said.

"Why were you screaming and yelling?"

"Oh, it's silly, Grandpa," Lana started to explain. "I wanted to see if the cooler would float in the water. It did, but then it went so fast. We tried to catch it and got all wet."

I didn't say a word but nodded in agreement to Lana's almost lie.

"I'm sorry we lost your cooler, Grandpa," Lana said and went to give him a hug, but he pushed her away. "You're all wet and muddy. Go and clean up before Grandma wakes up."

After we put on clean clothes, Lana was quieter than usual. Then she gave me a hug and whispered, "Lori, you saved my life."

I was surprised. First that Lana would give me a hug. She didn't like to be touched—except maybe by her mom and dad. "I feel too squished," she complained.

Then I saw tears in her eyes.

"Lana," I said and patted her back. I was embarrassed. "I didn't do anything."

"Yes, you did!" She pulled away. "I would have drowned in that cooler if you hadn't rescued me."

"Oh," I giggled. "The water wasn't that deep—you would have gotten out by yourself."

"It got deep in the cooler!" she exclaimed.

"Yeah, but . . ." I protested.

"You saved my life!" she said firmly and stomped out of the house.

7. Moon of New Names

After the adventure with the foam cooler, we were forbidden to play at the creek. It was a hot summer, and I missed the water, but Lana didn't seem to. She behaved herself and rarely was scolded. She didn't have to be told to be quiet or slow down, and she was nice to me. She believed I had saved her life.

"Is the TV too loud?" she asked as I read my book.

She even offered to help pull weeds in my garden row. She didn't do anything to get her or me into trouble.

One evening our family and Shoua and her parents were having a cookout in Grandpa's yard. Fresh sweet corn was bubbling in a big pot over a campfire. Dad grilled hamburgers to eat with the salads and other good stuff each family brought.

While we waited for the food to cook, Mrs. Vang said, "Shoua, show Lori and Lana the girl game you learned in the camp." She gave Shoua a handful of rubber bands.

"Okay," Shoua said. She gave each of us some rubber bands and showed us how to connect them into a long rope. "The girls in camp played this jumping game," she explained. Then she began to swing the string of rubber bands over her head and tried to jump over before it hit her feet.

"You try," she said, handing the string of rubber bands to me. The rubber bands were floppy and wanted to flip around my wrists. The string wasn't as easy to use as one of our firmer ropes. I didn't jump very well and was all out of breath when I handed the rubber bands to Lana.

Lana swung the string over and back a few times and then easily and gracefully jumped, faster and faster. She would have kept going, but one of her braids caught the rubber bands and she had to stop.

"Ooh!" I seethed to myself as everyone clapped at Lana's performance. She always had to be the best. Our moms were next and giggled like girls as they tried to jump.

I wandered to the porch where Grandpa had his flutes displayed on the porch. He was one of the few Indian men who still knew how to fashion Lakota flutes that were beautiful in their tone and form.

Mr. Vang had a reed pipe that had been made by an uncle in Laos. He told us, "It is a *cha mblay*. It used to be played by young people." He blew into it, and a soft sound filled the air. "The lovers had a coded melody to tell each other about their feelings."

Then he showed us a bamboo flute. "This is a *queej*," he said, making the word sound like *quing*. "Men play this." He blew a jumpy sounding tune.

When Mr. Vang stopped playing, Grandpa held up one of his flutes.

"What is the bird over the reed?" Mr. Vang asked.

"It is a wood pecker. We have a legend that it showed us how to make a flute. One pecked holes in a cedar branch. The wind began to blow, and as the wood pecker stepped on the holes, music was heard."

"Is this also a bird?" Mr. Vang asked, pointing to the open end of the flute.

"Yes," Grandpa answered. "It is a water bird, like a crane or duck. It depends on what the flute maker chooses. When these birds migrate, there is always one that is the leader, showing the way. So, the image on the flute shows the way to young lovers."

Grandpa blew softly, and a plaintive melody filled the evening air.

"These flutes were used for courting," Grandpa explained. "A young man would stand outside of his sweetie's tipi. If she liked the music she would take her blanket and go to meet him. If her parents approved they didn't stop her. The couple would wrap themselves in the blanket and stand close until her mother told her to come back inside."

Grandpa and Mr. Vang played their flutes at the same time. Some of the notes sounded the same; others made us cover our ears. "Ooh, you need to practice," said Mom. "Come on now, it's time to eat.

The Vangs enjoyed corn on the cob. "The grain we usually eat is rice. But this is good," Mrs. Vang said to Grandma.

After the meal Grandpa asked, "Is it okay if I take the kids with me tomorrow? I have flutes to deliver to Mount Rushmore and Crazy Horse Monument."

Our parents gave him permission. "Keep an eye on Chuckie," they reminded Lana and I, "and don't be any trouble for Grandma and Grandpa."

"Can Shoua come?" I asked, and her parents agreed, also cautioning her to be good.

The next morning we got out of our parents' cars and into Grandpa's. Chuckie had to ride in his car seat, but Lana didn't complain about the backseat being crowded. She sat next to him, and Shoua sat by the window so that she could better see the scenery. I sat in front between Grandma and Grandpa.

"We're going up a mountain," Shoua cried as Grandpa tromped on the accelerator going up the steep road. "Why are they called the 'Black Hills'?" she wanted to know.

"Because," Lana explained, "our ancestors thought they looked black when they came from the prairie. But it was the spruce trees so close together that looked dark."

Grandpa drove into the parking lot at Mount Rushmore, and Grandpa and Grandma went to the gift shop with the flutes. At the end of a long, paved walkway loomed the huge faces of the four presidents. The flags of every state of the nation and of the territories lined the way. Shoua and I tried to guess what state each flag represented before we read the sign at the base of the pole.

"Oh, come on," Lana remarked impatiently. "You're too slow. We won't have time to walk the trail."

She and Chuckie led the way up the walk that led to the trail under the four presidents. "They don't look very impressive," Shoua said and giggled as we looked up to see giant chins and noses.

Lana stood on a bench and climbed up onto the railing along the trail. "Some Indians don't think they should be up there at all," Lana said as she balanced on the narrow board.

"Why?" Shoua asked.

"Lana, get down. You might fall," I scolded her.

"I'm okay," she said and then explained to Shoua, "George Washington was known as an Indian fighter before he was the first president."

"Thomas Jefferson," she went on, "sent Lewis and Clark to explore Indian lands—then all the white people came. Teddy Roosevelt took more Indian land and made parks.

"Abe Lincoln hung Indians in Minnesota," Lana said as she balanced on the railing.

"Wait a minute, kids," a deep voice called to us. We turned to see a tall man lift Chuckie down to the trail. "Good thing your legs can't reach the railing."

The man towered over us. With his ranger hat silhouetted against the sky, we couldn't see his face until he turned. Then we saw braids hanging over the shoulders of his uniform.

"What—?" Lana said and then teetered, losing her balance.

The ranger grabbed her arm and then lifted her down to the trail. "This is where you supposed to walk," he said. "If you fell from here you'd be lucky if you just broke an arm or leg. Is this your brother?" he asked, pointing to Chuckie, who was clutching my hand and crying.

Lana nodded.

"You'd better keep a better eye on him—all of you," he warned, motioning to Shoua and me.

"Yes, sir," Lana said.

"And don't climb on the railing again."

"No, sir, I won't," Lana promised. She knelt down by Chuckie. "Shh, don't cry. It's okay."

"I'm sorry if I scared you," the ranger said as he smiled and patted Chuckie's head. "Come on down to the ice cream store, I'll get you a treat." He sat Chuckie on his shoulders.

"Whee," Chuckie shouted—he liked being up high.

"Thank you," we all said to Mr. Baker, who waved and walked to his office.

Grandma and Grandpa found us eating ice cream on the patio under the rock faces. We explained about the ranger.

"He's nice," Chuckie said. "He's big. He carried me all the way down."

Grandma and Grandpa smiled at each other. "That's Gerad Baker, the superintendent of the monument. He's a member of the Mandan-Hidatsa tribe. We're all so proud that an American Indian has such an important job," Grandma said. "He wants Mount Rushmore to be a meeting place for all the different cultures that live in the United States."

"He makes sure that the Indian view is expressed and that our art is authentically Indian-made," Grandpa said. "It's a good place for my flutes." Then he turned to Lana with a sigh.

"Lana, you could have been badly injured if you fell. And you didn't set a good example for your brother."

"I'm sorry," Lana replied sincerely.

"And you two," he said, turning to Shoua and me, "shouldn't have let her do it!"

"Yeah, sure," I thought, "like Lana listens to me!" But I apologized along with Shoua.

We left Mount Rushmore and drove to Crazy Horse Monument. Grandpa told Shoua and Chuckie about the Lakota hero who was being sculpted on the granite mountain.

"He was the Lakota's greatest leader. He led warriors to many victories over the U.S. Army. He fought to keep his people's land. But he finally had to go with the other Indians into the fort. There he was arrested. He tried to escape and was killed.

"We Lakota are proud of him. He was not afraid to die for his freedom."

I gazed up at the mountain and listened quietly while Grandpa talked. We walked over to the tipi on the veranda of the visitors' center.

"It's sort of small," Shoua noted. "How could a whole family live in one?"

"This is a small tipi. It's like the one that might be used when hunting," explained a young Indian man who was dressed in dance regalia. "There's a large one in the main building."

We sat on benches and watched as the young man and other Indians danced for the tourists. Then we joined in the round dance with other children, stepping in time to the drum.

"That was fun," Shoua said.

"Let's get some lunch," Grandpa said. I turned to follow him. "Where's Lana?" he asked.

I looked around but didn't see her. Mrs. Ziolkowski, whose husband had started the sculpture, walked by. We called her Mrs. Z. She saw Grandpa and came over to shake his hand.

"Have you brought more flutes for the gift shop?" she asked.

Grandpa nodded, "I just took five to the shop. But now we're looking for Lana."

"Uh, oh" Mrs. Z. chuckled, "I hope she's not trying get a goat again."

"I hope not," Grandpa said. "That girl can sure get into trouble."

They were talking about an earlier incident when Lana and I were about six years old. I was busy eating an ice cream cone while my grandparents were in the gift shop. Grandma noticed that the tourists were pointing to the base of carving. We looked and saw several wild goats in the rocks. We watched them for a while.

"Look! There's a little girl climbing up to the goats," someone shouted.

It was Lana trying to get to the goats. A security guard drove a jeep up to get her. Mrs. Z. was very upset. "How did she manage to get up there?" she wondered. "It's a long walk."

Lana really got in trouble then, so now Mrs. Z. told us, "I'll call security to look for her."

But she didn't have to because one of the guards came out of the museum with Lana.

"Found her sleeping in the big tipi," he explained.

We had walked past the big tipi and looked in. It was furnished like an old-time tipi would have been on the plains.

"The buffalo robe was so soft," Lana explained. "I meant to sit for just a minute . . . but I guess I fell asleep."

"Didn't you see the sign? I asked. "People aren't supposed to go in the tipi?"

Lana yawned. "I was tired after the dancing," she answered. Then she saw that Grandpa was upset, so she said, "I'm sorry, Mrs. Z., I didn't touch anything but the robe. I won't ever do it again, I promise."

Mrs. Z. gave Lana a quick hug—forgiving her like most people did.

"Now," Grandpa said, "let's have lunch."

We had buffalo stew in the Laughing Water Café. I was hungry and didn't notice that Lana wasn't eating much. She usually ate twice as fast and twice as much as I did.

"Aren't you hungry?" Grandma asked Lana, who seemed to stir the stew more than she ate it.

"Not really," Lana said. "I'm sort of tired."

"Well, you girls talk so much after you go to bed," Grandpa teased, because he had to tell us to go to sleep last night.

"I'm not tired," I said. "I wish we could dance some more with the kids out by the small tipi. I like the round dance. That was fun."

"So did I," said Shoua.

"Me too," agreed Chuckie.

"Well, eat up. We'll have to get you girls home and early to bed. Grandma's got more things for us to do for the naming ceremony."

The next day was Saturday, and our mothers drove to look at fabric for the special ribbon dresses we would wear at the ceremony. Shoua went too and helped us choose pretty calico prints and ribbons. "Why do they have to wear ribbon dresses?" she wanted to know.

"In the old days, before Indians learned how to sew cotton material," Mom explained, "a girl would have a new buckskin dress for her naming ceremony. But after the Indians lived on reservations and could no longer hunt the way they used to, it was difficult to get hides to tan for clothing. So the women learned to use sewing machines and made dresses from fabric.

"The dresses were made much the same as if the material were buckskin, but they looked very plain because there was no leather to fringe them. So some woman began trimming the dresses with bright ribbons, and ribbon dress became a new part of our tradition."

As the day of the naming neared, Grandma told us what to expect at the ceremony. "Mr. Iron Shell will be the *Wicasa Wakan*, the holy man who will conduct the Lakota ceremony. Father Jim will lead the prayers from the church. When they speak you must listen very carefully. Be respectful and pay attention. Don't look around at your friends. Everyone will be watching you."

That made me a little bit scared. "Oh, I hope we don't do something stupid," I stated, meaning I hoped Lana wouldn't. "There'll be so many people looking."

To my surprise Lana agreed. "Yeah, it'll be terrible if they laughed at us!" We would have to behave, or we would shame our family, who had worked so hard for this ceremony.

The day before the ceremony, Grandma's kitchen was crowded with people who were helping prepare the food for the celebration. Shoua and her mom helped, and we all peeled, sliced, and chopped vegetables for the stew that would be served. Mom and Aunt Martha mixed the dough for the bread that would be fried early next morning so that it would be fresh. Dad stirred the *wojape*—the chokecherry pudding—so that it wouldn't scorch and taste bad.

Uncle Joe made gallons of lemonade and let Chuckie and Grandpa taste it to make sure it was sweet enough. At the end of the day, everyone was tired but pleased that everything was ready.

It seemed as if I had just fallen asleep when Mom woke me and announced, "Take your shower and shampoo your hair. You need to be clean for the ceremony."

All the food and giveaway items were loaded into cars and taken to the community hall. As I got out of the car, I saw that many people had already arrived.

It was time. The drum boomed, the people stood, the singers began the flag song, and the color guard marched into the hall followed by the *Wicasa Wakan* and Father Jim. First Father Jim prayed in English, then the *Wicasa Wakan* prayed in Lakota. Both asked for special blessings on all the people and especially for Lana and I.

Mr. Iron Shell explained the purpose of the ceremony: "These girls are being honored by their grandparents with Lakota names that they will have the rest of their lives." He motioned for us to come forward. Lana grabbed my hand, and I knew she was as nervous as I was and glad that we were together and not all alone in front of so many people. Mr. Iron Shell directed us to sit in chairs in the center of the room. One chair was covered with Lana's quilt, and a second with mine. Then I realized that there was a third chair covered with a quilt. Lana noticed too, and we looked at each other and then saw Grandma and Grandpa bringing Shoua onto the floor. They smiled at us, and Shoua was grinning even as tears ran down her face.

"We adopt Shoua Vang as our granddaughter," Grandpa said.

"Lori and Lana wanted her to be a 'blood sister,' and so we make her a member of our family," Grandma said.

We squeezed Shoua's hands and sat on the chairs.

We watched Mr. Iron Shell place the ceremonial items by the buffalo skull altar and listened as he prayed that we would be good women and honor our people.

"Pejuta Okawin." He spoke my new name and handed Grandpa an eagle plume medicine wheel that he fastened to my hair. "Skanskanwin," he said to Lana, and Grandma tied the medicine wheel in her hair.

"Because Shoua has the beautiful eyes of a doe, we name her

Tahca Istawin," Grandpa said, and Grandma put the wheel in her hair.

The ceremony was over. The drum boomed, and the singers began the honor song. We stood, and Grandma and Grandpa embraced us. Then our parents gave us hugs and led us to the dance floor. At first we danced alone, and then family and friends came to shake our hands or give us a hug and joined the dance.

"The family of these girls," Mr. Iron Shell announced, "wish to present gifts in their honor." First we gave the quilts, the most valued items to be given away, to the people who were most important to the ceremony—Mr. Iron Shell, Father Jim, and the singers. Then we gave away the other things so that everyone had a gift. Each recipient shook our hands and thanked us for the gift.

Father Jim stood and blessed the food, and we helped take plates of food to the old people who couldn't stand in the serving line. We made sure that everyone had food before we ate. Finally, Father Jim said, "The family asked me to express their thanks to Mr. Iron Shell, the singers, and to all friends and relatives who helped with the ceremony and to all who joined us for this special occasion. *Pilamiye*."

8. Moon When the Buffalo Run

Shortly after we got our new names, school began.

It was hard to sit in the classroom and concentrate on schoolwork. The autumn days were sunny and warm. Green trees became vividly gold and rust and glowed among dark pines. It was an awesome Indian summer and perfect for the annual Buffalo Roundup in Custer State Park. We were eager to go, but first Grandpa took us to the *Tatanka* sculpture. *Tatanka* means buffalo in Lakota, and the bronze sculpture depicted huge buffalos being chased by Indians on horseback.

The many figures seemed so alive I could almost hear the horses' neighs, the hunters' shouts, and the roar of the buffalo as they plummeted over the cliff.

Grandpa explained, "I wanted you to see this before the roundup to give you an idea of what a buffalo hunt might have been like. This is how hunters could kill much more game than they could by shooting one at a time with a bow and arrows."

I thought it was cruel. "You mean they deliberately chased the buffalo over the cliff?"

"It's called a jump, and yes, they stampeded as many as they could over it."

I shivered at the thought.

Grandpa said, "You must remember that the people would starve if the hunters didn't kill as many buffalo as they could. The buffaloes not only provided food, but hides made tipis, moccasins, and storage containers, and the bones were made into tools and toys. The buffalo was at the center of the tribe's life."

We were quiet listening to Grandpa, even Lana. I had expected her to want to climb the sculptures, but she just gazed at them.

The next day we went to the festival that was held before the roundup. This was the third time Lana and I got to go. The roundup was early Monday morning, and we had to be excused from school.

We got out of the car at the campground and heard music. The foot-tapping sound of fiddles, banjos, guitars, and singers pulled us toward the colorful awnings and white tents of the nearby arts festival.

"Ooh," Shoua breathed, "it all looks so perfect!"

The bright colors of the canvas bloomed in the green pines, glittering golden aspen, and red sumac of the forest.

"Come on," Lana yelled and ran toward the music.

"Whoa," Uncle Joe called. "First, we set up camp, and then we play."

"Well, hurry up!" Lana replied as she rushed to the van and started tossing out sleeping bags.

"Calm down, Lana," Aunt Martha cautioned. "There's plenty of time for fun."

It didn't take us long to set up the four tents. We three girls had wanted our own tent, but our parents decided that we wouldn't get any sleep together, and we had to get up early for the round-up. So I helped Mom and Dad set up our domed tent. Lana, Chuckie, Aunt Martha, and Uncle Joe had one that poked up like an umbrella, and Mr. and Mrs. Vang and Shoua were in a long, triangle-shaped tent. Grandma and Grandpa's tent was the last to be set up.

At last we were free. Chuckie wanted to come with us, but Dad and Uncle Joe took him to see the horses. We raced away and then had to slow to a walk through the crowded lanes between the booths of glittering jewelry, gleaming pottery, baskets, hats, sweatshirts, and moccasins.

Boom! We covered our ears to loud blasts. They were coming from guns fired by men in fringed buckskin in the black powder shooting competition. Beyond the firing range, tipis ringed the outer edge of the festival grounds.

"Lana," we heard, "wait up." It was Andy Brown Wolf. He was dressed like an old-time Indian would have—his bare chest under a leather vest and wearing leggings and moccasins—but he had on briefs under his loincloth.

"What are you doing, Andy?" we asked.

"My parents and I are part of the Indian reenactors' camp. I'm helping my cousin Burdette. He makes flint-knapped arrowheads. He's teaching me how to make them. Come see our tipi," he said, taking Lana's hand.

Shoua and I followed them. We saw buckskin-clad Indians demonstrating how to make hand drums, buffalo-horn spoons, arrowheads, and spears. Others tanned hides, made moccasins, and dried corn and berries. Crowds gathered to watch a large tipi being erected.

We sat on the ground and watched as men, women, and children who were all dressed in dance regalia demonstrated the steps to traditional dances. Then we joined in the round dance with other children, stepping in time to the drum.

"That was fun," Shoua said, sort of out of breath.

"Yeah," I agreed, "but now I'm hungry."

I got buffalo jerky and *wasna*. Then I bought fry bread and took it with us to the chili cook off, where competing cooks gave us spicy hot samples.

I took a big bite and gasped. "That's too hot!" I said.

"I don't think so," Shoua said in between spoonfuls of chili.

"You can have mine." I handed her the little cup. "I think I'll have a buffalo burger," I said, and I looked around for the burger stands. Then I noticed that Lana wasn't with us.

"Now, where'd she go?" I complained. Our parents had told us to stay together, but leave it to Lana to do what she wanted.

"Don't know," Shoua answered, looking around. "Last I saw her she was with Andy."

"We better go back and look for her."

It was quiet at the tipi site. The dancers were taking a break, and we walked all over the area but didn't see Lana or Andy.

We found Burdette, but he hadn't seen Lana either. But he led us to an area behind the tipis where pickups and vans were parked among the trees, and there was Lana.

She was sitting in a camp chair drinking a bottle of water. Andy sat at her feet.

"Where have you been?" I demanded. "We've been looking all over for you!"

"I was thirsty," Lana explained. "I asked Andy for water. Next thing I knew he was shaking me. I saw him and the others all in leather . . . and the tipis . . . I wasn't sure where I was. I thought I'd died and gone to the ancestors."

"That's silly," I said. I thought she was trying to be funny, even though she wasn't smiling.

"She seemed confused," Mrs. Brown Wolf said. "She told us where you are camped, and I was about to send Andy to tell her folks, then you girls came."

"Well, you better come now," I grumbled. "The festival will close soon, and we have to go back to camp."

"Okay." Lana stood and sort of swayed like she was dizzy. Shoua took her arm. But Lana moved away. "Thanks for the water, Mrs. Brown Wolf."

"I'll come with you," Andy said, taking Lana's other arm.

We slowly made our way through the departing crowds to our tents. The adults scolded us for being late, but after we told them about Lana fainting, they made her sit and fussed over her.

"Bye Andy," Lana waved. "See you tomorrow."

Supper was ready. It was Grandma's yummy venison stew and fry bread. I was hungry and didn't notice that Lana wasn't eating much.

"Aren't you hungry?" Grandma asked Lana, who was stirring more than eating. She usually ate twice as fast and twice as much as I did.

"Did you have too much fry bread?"

"No," Lana said. "I'm sort of tired."

"It's been a busy afternoon," Grandma acknowledged. "So I'm not surprised."

"I'm not tired," I said. "Can we go dance some more over by the tipis? Burdette said they'd have round dances this evening. That'll be fun."

"Oh, let's sit and watch the fire," Mom said. "We don't get to do this very often."

All of us sat around the fire, soothed by the flickering flames.

"Tell me about tomorrow," I asked Grandpa. "Why is there a buffalo roundup?"

"Bison," Grandpa corrected, "that's what they are. The park area can't feed more than a thousand head of bison. There's only so much grazing available. So each fall the rangers and volunteers round up fifteen hundred or more bison and head them to the confined area down there near the corrals. They're vaccinated against disease and separated by age. The yearlings are sold off."

"Who buys them and why?"

"Ranchers and others who want to add to or start a bison herd."

"Mr. Vang," Lana asked, "did you hunt buffalo in Laos?"

"No," Mr. Vang smiled. "No, we didn't have bison. We hunted deer, wild pig, pheasant, and another bird we called 'jungle chicken.'"

"What kind of weapon did you have?" Dad asked.

"My father hunted with a crossbow. I had a rifle when I was four-teen, but I didn't use it for hunting." He paused, remembering.

"I was recruited by your country to join the *armée clan-destine.*"

"What's that?" I asked.

"It's French," Mom said.

Mr. Vang nodded. "It means 'secret army.' Hmong soldiers were trained in guerrilla warfare to fight against the North Viet-namese. We directed air strikes for American pilots and rescued downed flyers. We reported on where the enemy was."

"Was this during the Vietnam War?" Dad asked. "We were there," he said, nodding to Uncle Joe. "We never heard of Hmong soldiers."

"It was secret," Mr. Vang explained. "After the war, some of our officers were evacuated to the U. S., but the rest of us had to hide from the Communists, who wanted to kill us all."

"That sounds like what happened to our people," my dad said. We all sat quietly watching the fire until Chuckie asked, "Grand-pa, did you ever hunt buffalo like the Indians did?"

Everyone smiled, and Grandpa chuckled.

"No, Chaske. Not like the old-time Indians did. My grandpa, the first to be named High Elk, was the last to hunt buffalo. He said that he hunted them after the Battle of Greasy Grass—what the white men called Custer's Last Stand.

"After the battle the tribes scattered because they knew the troopers would be after them to avenge the deaths of Custer and his men. The band camped in the area of what is now called Slim Buttes. The older boys were sent to hunt while the war-riors guarded the camp.

"High Elk and two friends rode a half day from camp and stopped at a stream to water and rest their horses.

"The three kept a sharp eye on the hills around them. None said it, but Grandpa told me that they were afraid—not fearful of the enemy, but of failing to bring meat to their hungry families.

"Suddenly the horses snorted and backed out of the water. The boys had to grab the reins to keep their mounts from bolting.

"Then they heard a lowing, bawling sound—it was buffalo.

"One of the boys walked quietly through the scrub trees around the bend in the stream and saw three cows, an old bull, and some calves. He signaled to the others, who quickly took places to shoot. They decided to all aim at the nearest cow—they didn't dare miss and waste ammunition.

"High Elk said he had to make himself take slow, deep breaths to steady his hands. His friend counted *wanzi*, *nonpa*, and at *yamni* they shot.

"But just as they did, the bull moved in front of the cow. The boys were stunned. They knew the bullets had struck, but the bull didn't go down. Its massive head swung slowly toward them.

"Frantically, they tried to reload when the huge beast took a step and fell with a muffled thump that made the ground tremble. It was dead.

"The rest of the small herd left and the boys went to their kill. High Elk said they sang to the dead bull, praising his strength and thanking him for giving his life for the people.

"High Elk and one other friend began butchering the animal, while the third rode back to get help. The beast was too big for three boys to manage.

"Late in the afternoon, the families of the three young men and others of the small band made camp at the stream. The women finished the butchering and soon had the tongue and hump simmering for their first meal in many days.

"Not only did the buffalo feed the hungry people, but because he was too big for three boys to handle, the band moved to the creek and found safety in the sheltered place. This small group escaped the death that came to the rest of their band, who were killed by U.S. troops.

"So that was my grandpa's last buffalo hunt."

Over the stillness that fell after Grandpa ended his story, we could hear drum beats from the dances at the tipis.

"Now," Grandma said quietly, "let's go to bed."

I could see Grandpa's story in my mind and fell asleep to the distant beat of the drums and high trills of the singers.

Something woke me in the darkest time of night—I wasn't sure when. Then I heard the *huun huu* of an owl from the forest. Its eerie call made me pull my sleeping bag over my head.

I awoke again to Dad's hand on my arm. "Get up Lori. It's time."

It was so early and still dark, and I snuggled back into my warm sleeping bag. I liked to camp, but I hated having to get up in the cold. I heard Shoua ask, "Is Grandpa all right?"

"Sure," Grandpa answered. "I'm just fine. Just a bit stiff from sleeping on the ground."

"Come on Shoua, sit by me in the car," Lana said.

I crawled quickly out of the bag and dressed, shivering in the damp chill.

We climbed in the cars and drove off to the park corrals, where the buffalo would come. By the time we drove through the gate the sun was up. Dad drove slowly, following the car ahead, and was directed to pull into a parking place. We three girls and our parents took folding chairs and blankets to a high area set aside for viewing the roundup. Andy showed up and sat on the ground by Lana's chair. We waited.

The grown-ups had coffee and gave us hot chocolate to drink with the granola bars we'd brought for breakfast.

"This is the first time I've been to a breakfast picnic," Shoua remarked.

"Me too," Chuckie said.

"Did you like being in a sleeping bag?" I asked Shoua. This was her first camping trip.

"Oh, it was so warm and cozy. I slept real hard until the owl woke me up."

"I heard it too," I said.

"Did it scare you?" Shoua asked.

"It gave me goose bumps and—"

Suddenly, people all around us stood and pointed, shouting, "There they are!"

We strained to see a dark clump moving down the hill.

"More over there!" someone else cried.

"There's more!"

Now we could see smaller, moving dark spots of buffalo being herded together. Horseback riders and drivers in 4-wheel-drive pickups were directing the buffalo. Some of the pickups had tv cameras in them that were difficult to hold steady as the vehicles bounced over the rough terrain. A high, sturdy fence separated the furious dash from the spectators.

Some of the buffalo tried to turn against the flow of the herd. One broke away and ran down a draw. Two riders went after it, but the buffalo was faster, and we all cheered as it raced over the hill.

"That old bull," Grandpa chuckled, "remembers what happens and wants no part of it. Look! There's another trying to break out!"

"Here they come!"

The ground trembled and dust rose under thousands of hooves thundering toward us. Birds, rabbits, squirrels, and even a coyote fled before the rushing beasts.

"Oh, oh!!" we screamed, thrilled and excited at the amazing sight of this living, fluid mass flowing down one hill and up another. Then it was finished. The bison slowed to a walk and calmly moved through a gate to the confinement pasture. They milled about and then lowered their heads to feed on the tall grass.

"It's over again," Grandpa said.

9. Moon When the Leaves Blow Off

The warm, Indian summer days changed to days of cold wind that swirled leaves across the lawn and into the street in front of the school.

We weren't the only children who had been excused from school to go to the Buffalo Roundup. In the past, kids that didn't go to the roundup asked so many questions that the teachers now had ten minutes at the start of the day for "Roundup Reports."

We each told what we liked best and what we liked least about the roundup.

"The best part was the huge herd of buffalo all running together," I reported. I had to think hard about what I didn't like, but I finally said, "I didn't like getting out of my warm sleeping bag so early in the morning."

Shoua had a harder time deciding what was best. "It was *all* wonderful, but the running buffalo was the most exciting," she decided and sat down.

"What didn't you like?" asked the teacher.

Shoua frowned, "Hmm, I guess hearing the owl in the night. It was scary."

"Why was it scary?

"Because the last time I heard a bird at night was in the camp in Thailand. My dad said it was *Dav Liv Nyug*, the evil bird. It is bigger and louder than an owl, but it hoots the same. We believe that when we hear it at midnight, someone will die. The next morning my grandpa died. It brings bad news."

"Did you have any bad news this time?"

Shoua shook her head. "No, but I was afraid that Grandpa High Elk had died." She looked at me and smiled. "But he didn't."

Grandpa came to get us after school, and we told him about the owl.

"I heard it too," I said. But I didn't think it was hooting bad news.

Grandpa said, "The Lakota and other tribes believe that an owl's call is preparing the hearer for bad news or announcing the death of a loved one."

"Well," said Lana, "there hasn't been any bad news, and nobody died. So this owl didn't mean anything."

"Shoua," Lana said, changing the subject, "are you going to the powwow with us?" She was referring to the upcoming event when Indians get together to dance in competitions and for one another.

"Yes," Shoua answered. "My parents and I will go with your family."

"Good," I said. "The powwow is fun and exciting, and we can dance too."

On the first night of the powwow, we arrived early to get good seats and to be in time to watch the grand entry of all the men, women, and children who would dance in the powwow.

First came the Honor Guard of U. S. Military Veterans in the uniforms of their branch of service. They carried the flags of the United States and of South Dakota. Behind them were men and women who carried the flags of each Indian reservation in the state. They all marched to the center of the arena, stepping in time to the beat of the drum.

The dancers came after the Honor Guard and circled the flags. The elder grandpas and grandmas entered with slow, stately steps. The Grass Dancers, whose costumes had long fringes that swayed like grass in the wind, followed them.

"There's Andy!" Lana yelled and waved. He waved back and stepped higher, stomped harder, and spun faster than the others around him.

Over the boom of the drum, ankle bells twinkled and tinkled and the women's shawls fluttered like wings. Other women in buckskin dresses stepped sedately to the drum's beat, their shawls draped over one arm. More men, women, boys, and girls moved to the drum beat until the arena floor was a bobbing, swaying sea of bright colors.

There was a small gap between the dancers then a group of young women and little girls entered the hall. At each step little tin cones on the satiny dresses sparkled as they clinked together.

"Ooh," Lana said, "listen to the *swishklinging*!"

"It sounds like *jinglingling* to me," I said.

"*Swishklinging*," Lana insisted. "The cones swish together when the dancers move, and they jingle at the same time. *Swishklinging*."

I didn't want to argue with her. I was stunned by all the colors, the movement, and the sounds of the grand entry procession.

Gradually, the dancers left the floor, and it was almost quiet as the dance competitions began. There were the men's traditional and Grass Dancers competitions, women's traditional, and so on. In between the sets were the intertribal dances in which anyone could dance. Lana, Shoua, and I proudly wore the shawls that Grandma had made for us. We led the way to the dance floor. Andy came to dance with Lana, Shoua and I followed, and then Grandma and Mrs. Vang and Mom and Aunt Martha stepped together. Our dads only danced the first set—they said it was more fun to watch and hard to step in cowboy boots.

I was out of breath from the excitement and fun of the dance. It was hot, and we were glad to sit and have a drink of water. But I was ready to dance when the drum sounded.

Mom and Aunt Martha wanted to sit this dance out, so I called to Lana and Shoua, "Come on, let's dance."

Lana took my hand as we walked down the steps to the

arena floor. She had started to move with the other dancers when she grabbed my arm.

"I got to sit," she panted.

This wasn't like Lana, who usually ran circles around me at anything. But I said, "Oh, go sit down then. I'm going to dance!"

But she clutched Shoua's arm. "Oh," she said, "it's so hot!"

"Come on," I griped, "I'll take you back to your seat. She was panting and sweating after climbing the steps.

"I'll help her," said Andy.

Shoua and I walked back to the floor and moved around it with the other dancers.

We were back in our seats when we heard, "Jingle dancers, come to the floor!"

I poked Lana because this was our favorite event.

The young dancers stood straight and tall, left hands on their hips. In their right hands were feather fans. The drums boomed, the men sang, and the dancers flowed over the floor to the rhythmic beat.

The song was sung through several times, then it stopped and the dancers slowly raised their feather fans above their heads in the "honor beat." There was a pause before the drum and song began again and the dancers moved.

I loved the story of the jingle dresses. The announcer told it as the dance began:

"Long ago on an Ojibwe reservation, a father was worried about his daughter, who was very ill. He thought about her all of the time, even in his sleep. One night he dreamed that he rolled tobacco can lids into cones. Then his mother sewed them on a dress for the little girl.

"The father remembered his dream after he woke. He knew that his dead mother, the little girl's grandma, had sent him a message. He gathered hundreds of lids from men of the tribe and made the cones. The girl's mother made a special dress and sewed the cones to it.

"The little girl put on the dress, and as she danced, she grew stronger, the illness left her, and she was well.

"She wore the dress and danced at a reservation gathering.

"Other girls liked the dress and wanted one. So their grandmothers made them dresses while their grandfathers or fathers made the cones."

We listened to the story and watched the dancers. Our feet tapped, and our heads bobbed to the drum beat. We didn't want them to stop, but the dance ended. It was time to go home.

On the way out of the arena we walked through many exhibits where vendors sold brightly beaded and gleaming turquoise earrings, shawls, and dance regalia. Then we saw jingle dresses.

I pulled on Dad's hand. "Could I have a jingle dress?" I begged. "They're beautiful."

"Oh, I'd love to have one," Lana said, "and Shoua needs one, too."

Our parents looked at the dresses and at the price tags. "No," my dad said, "they are too expensive."

"No," Lana's mother said, "they cost too much."

"Can I have one if I save my babysitting money?" I asked.

"We'll see," said Dad.

"I'll save my newspaper money," said Lana, who had started delivering the local paper.

"It will take forever to save enough money for that one," I noted, pointing to a bright blue satin dress with gleaming rows of jingles that seemed to shimmer with their own lights.

"I can save it," Lana bragged.

"I bet you can't," I said.

"Stop arguing," Lana's mother commanded, and she led the way out of the arena.

Lana glared at me. I snapped my eyes at her.

"You're both tired," Grandma said, moving between us and taking our hands.

We didn't forget about the jingle dresses, and even when we weren't together we chatted about them. Our parents had computers that we were allowed to use for our homework. After the homework was done, we sent e-mails to each other.

> *Dear Lana,*
> I walked around two blocks in my neighborhood and left a note at each house. In it I printed, "Reliable baby sitter. Good rates and my phone number." To my surprise I got lots of calls. But Dad won't let me do it on weeknights.
> I'll never have enough money for a jingle dress.
> *Love, Lori*

Lana wrote back,

> I'm saving my paper money. I helped our neighbor rake leaves, and she paid me fifty cents. She said she'd hire me to shovel when the snow came. I know I'll have enough to get a dress.
> *Love, Lana*

"Lori," Dad called. "Shut down and turn out your lights."

I signed off.

10. Moon of the Hats

It stayed cold, and Lana had to quit her paper route. After coming home from the early morning delivery, she couldn't get warm, no matter how much hot chocolate she drank. But in the warm classroom, she'd fall asleep at her desk. When the teacher urged her to pay attention, Lana said, "Okay," but dozed off again.

The teacher called Aunt Martha and told her, "I'm concerned about Lana. She sleeps in class and doesn't eat much at lunchtime."

Lana's mother took her to the doctor. Lana later told us that a nurse poked a vein in her arm and filled many little bottles with blood. But she didn't sound as boastful as usual when she had done something I hadn't. Mom told us that Lana was very sick.

She had to go to a hospital in Denver for two weeks, and visitations were limited. The doctors didn't want her to get cold or flu germs that might make her sicker. Uncle Joe let her use his laptop in the hospital, so we sent e-mail.

Lana wrote:

> *Dear Lori,*
> The hospital is okay. I have my own room. Mom and Dad come to see me. Father Jim did too. They looked funny. They had to wear gowns. Put on masks and caps. They had booties on their feet. I have to have treatments. They don't hurt.
> But afterwards I feel yuk and don't want to eat. I never thought I would, but I miss school. Andy sends me e-mail too. Tell Shoua hi.
> *Love,*
> *Lana*

Lana didn't write about how sick she really was after the treatments, but I heard Mom telling Dad what Aunt Martha had said.

"Lana can hardly lift her hand, and she has to be fed. Or try to—she gets so nauseous and doesn't want to eat. It's so hard . . ." Mom sounded like she was going to cry.

Then I wrote to Lana and she replied.

> *Dear Lori,*
>
> Thank you for e-mail. Thank Shoua too. I'm glad she can use the computer at school. I have a room-mate. Her name is Sara. She has cancer too. There are other kids here too. We have fun in between treatments. Tell Shoua hi.
> *Love,*
> *Lana*

CANCER! I felt like I'd been punched. I knew Lana was really sick, but no one had used this word before. I showed the e-mail to Shoua, who started to cry and said, "That's the bad news the owl was hooting. Is she going to die?"

"NO!" I shouted. "Don't say that!"

Grandma heard me yelling and came from the kitchen.

"What?" she asked, and then she saw Shoua crying. "Have you girls had a fight?"

Shoua shook her head and wiped her tears. I handed Grandma the e-mail. "Lana has cancer," I whispered. "Is she going to die?"

Grandma pulled us down beside her on the couch. She put her arms around us. "We hope not," she said quietly. "When she comes back from Denver, she'll have more 'chemo' and radiation treatments in the hospital here. We're hoping that the disease will go into remission."

"What is that?" I asked.

"Remission is when the illness stops making Lana sick."

"Oh, like being cured."

"Sometimes there is a cure, but often the sickness stops for a long time but can come back again. If that happens, Lana will have to have more treatments. We need to hope and pray that Lana has remission and that it will last a long time."

> *Dear Lori,*
> I got in trouble. I bet you're not surprised. Sara and I challenged the boys across the hall to a race in our wheelchairs. The other kids cheered. The nurses made us quit. It was my idea—so I got a scolding. But it was fun. Sometimes it gets too grim here. Tell Shoua hi.
> *Love,*
> *Lana*

Aunt Martha told us what happened.

"Lana and her roommate were feeling pretty peppy and were allowed to 'cruise' in the hall. They met two boys who were also cruising, and Lana"—who else?—"suggested the race."

We laughed. She was the same daring Lana no matter where she was.

They might have gotten away with it, but other patients heard about the race and began choosing sides. The kids who could get out of bed watched from the doors of their rooms. One of them was the starter.

The boys were bigger and stronger and were soon ahead of the girls. But one bumped into the wall and lost control and ran into one of the bystanders. No one was hurt, but the nurses heard the laughter and cheers, which ended the competition. They asked the kids whose idea it was to race, and Lana admitted it was hers.

Dear Lori,
My treatments are done. The nurse says I'll get over
feeling rotten. But I look rotten now. My hair's fall-
ing out in gobs. And my head gets cold. I tie a scarf
on. I think I look funny. I'm glad you can't see me.
You'd laugh. Tell Shoua hi.
Love,
Lana

The kids at school had written "get well" and "come back soon"
letters to Lana. When they found out about her head being cold,
we had a bake sale. With the money we raised we sent her a jest-
er's hat and, at Christmas, a Santa Claus cap. She e-mailed a
thank you note to the school.

Dear Kids and Teachers,
Thank you for the hats. They keep my head warm. I
loan the one I'm not wearing to Sara. She's bald too.
I hope you don't mind. But no one sent her hats. We
both love the hats. Thanks again.
Love,
Lana

So we had another bake sale and bought hats for Sara.

Dear General Beadle School,
Thank you so much for the hats. I love them. Lana
and I wear the same ones. So we're like twins. Lana
is lots of fun. I'm glad she's my roommate.
Love,
Sara

11. Moon of the Dance

We had a white Christmas, and Lana was home but couldn't go to church. "Who carried the cross?" she asked.

"Andy did," I told her. "He held it high—he's getting tall."

Lana smiled. "Yeah. I was taller than him, but not anymore."

We teased Chuckie about his dance from last Christmas and laughed when he said that wasn't him—it was some other boy.

I went to see Lana every day, but some days she was too tired to do more than say hi.

Chuckie was glad to see me. He'd grab my hand and pull me to the sofa. "Lori, read me *Dancing*, please?" he begged. And I would, because I knew Lana couldn't do it and that Aunt Martha and Uncle Don were so busy looking after Lana and worrying about her that they kind of ignored Chuckie.

So we cuddled, and I read *Dancing Tepees*, and he looked at the beautiful pictures as I read the poems. He didn't want anything else. I guess it was the one thing that stayed the same in his house. All else had changed when Lana got sick.

"Don't go," he'd almost cry when I put my coat on to leave. So sometimes I took him home with me.

In the afternoon of Christmas Day we all went to Lana's house. She wore the Santa cap that matched her red pajamas. She was too weak to sit at the dining room table, so everyone ate in the living room, where Lana was on the sofa.

After dinner I helped Chuckie hand out the presents from under the tree. After they were all distributed, we took turns opening one package at a time. Chuckie went first. He opened the biggest one. "Cool," he cried and held up a big truck.

I don't remember what the others got, but most of my presents were books, while Lana got videos.

Then Grandma went to the closet. "Here are more gifts," she said. She held up two long, pink garment bags. She gave one to

Lana and the other to me. Then she helped Lana remove the pink bags.

"Oh, pretty!" Lana said in a voice that was louder and more excited than she'd used in a long time.

"A jingle dress!" we both cried.

"Try it on, Lori," Grandma said. "I hope it fits you girls. You've both gotten so tall . . ."

I went to the bedroom to put on the dress.

"Do you want to try on the dress?" Grandma asked Lana.

"Maybe later," Lana said and stroked the slick satin so that the cones jingled. "I'll see how it looks on Lori."

I loved the feel of the smooth satin as it slid over my head. I tried to move like the powwow dancers, so that jingles clinked together.

"You're *swishklinging*," Lana said.

I started to say they were *jinglingling* but then agreed, "Yeah," and twirled about the room.

"Did you make the dresses?" Lana asked Grandma.

"Yes," Grandma smiled, "and one for Shoua, too."

"Oh, thank you, Grandma," we both said, and I gave her a hug.

"You must thank Grandpa too," Grandma said. "He made the jingle cones."

"Thank you, Grandpa," we said, and I gave him a hug.

I swayed around the room. I watched myself in the mirror above the sofa and noticed how everyone was admiring me except for Lana. Then I felt terrible at such a thought.

Lana was too tired to watch. Uncle Joe carried her to her room. Her mother hung both jingle dresses on the outside of the closet door so Lana could admire them.

I dreamed about the jingle dresses. We were at the powwow—Lana, Shoua, and me. We stood straight and tall, left hands on our hips. In our right hands we each held a feather fan. The drums boomed and the men sang.

We were the only dancers. Our feet didn't touch the floor, and our movements flowed as one.

Then we were dancing as the buffalo ran, so many in one mass, sweeping down and up the hills. The drums beat louder and faster, and the buffalo tumbled over the jump. The jingles glittered and clinked more brightly. Lana smiled at the *swish-klinging* sound and soared above the stampede.

All day I kept thinking about my dream, of the dancing, and especially about the jingle dresses.

I called Shoua to tell her about my dream and the idea I had.

"Shoua, do you remember the story of the jingle dresses?"

"Yes. The father was worried about his sick daughter, and he thought about her so much that he had a dream."

"Just like I did," I said.

"Ohh, yeah," Shoua answered.

"So the father had the jingle dress made," I continued. "His little girl wore the dress and danced. She grew stronger, and she got well."

Shoua was quiet for a bit then asked, "Are you thinking of getting Lana to dance in her jingle dress?"

"Yes," I said, "but I need you to help me."

Shoua agreed. "I'll do anything. I want Lana to get well."

The next day I called Aunt Martha.

"Can Shoua and I come see Lana today? We could stay with her if you want to take Chuckie someplace."

"That will be very helpful, Lori. You could come right after lunch—say for thirty minutes or so, until Grandma gets here. Oh, Andy will be here too."

Lana was glad to see us. She was reclining on the sofa in red pajamas, the Santa hat on her head. Andy was on the floor.

"Hey, you two," she greeted. "See what Andy gave me for Christmas." In her hand was a small arrowhead. "He made it."

"Wow, Andy. You're getting to be a real 'knapper,'" I said.

"Thanks," he said shyly and then handed a picture to me. "This is what Lana gave me."

It was a drawing of Andy in his dance regalia. "That's really good," Shoua said.

"Yeah, Lana. Your drawing is great."

"I had lots of time to practice in the hospital," she said. "Want to watch the new movie I got for Christmas?"

"Maybe later, but Shoua wants to take a picture of the three of us in our jingle dresses."

"Yeah," Shoua said sadly, "to remember how much fun the three of us had." She swallowed a sob. "We're moving to Minneapolis."

"Oh, no!" Lana exclaimed. "That's terrible! When are you moving?"

"In January, so I can start school after the Christmas vacation." She smiled and wiped the tears away.

"So will you put on your jingle dress?"

"Do it," Andy urged Lana. "I'd like to see you wear it. I'll take the picture."

"Well, okay," Lana agreed. Shoua and I donned our dresses quickly and turned to help Lana.

"Come on," I said. "I am Pejuta Okawin, the medicine woman; this is part of your treatment. Put the dress over your pj's."

Andy held Lana upright while Shoua and I slid the dress over her head.

"Oops," Lana giggled. She grabbed her bald head as the Santa hat fell off. "Now you can see how ugly I am."

Shoua pulled the hat almost over Lana's nose. "You look better with your face covered." We all laughed.

Andy put his head close to Lana's ear and whispered something that made her blush and say, "Yeah sure. Pretty like a moose."

Andy straightened the hat, stepped back aiming the camera. "Okay, one, two, three, smile!" the camera flashed.

He helped steady Lana as I put the CD of powwow music in the player and forwarded to the track of the jingle dance song. "Oh, hear the *swishklinging*," Lana said to the sound of clinking jingles on the dancers. Soon drumming filled the room, and the singers' voices rose.

Shoua and I stood on either side of Lana. "Smile," Andy said and snapped the picture. He took one more.

"Come on, let's pretend we're at the powwow," I said.

Shoua and I stepped to the beat, but Lana didn't move until Andy steadied her with his arm around her waist. She leaned on him, and we moved around the room slowly, not quite in time to the drum—but Lana was dancing. Then she sagged to the floor.

"Lana!" Andy cried. "I'm sorry."

"You didn't drop me," she sighed. "I can't—my legs won't hold me."

"That's okay," I said. "Rest a bit, and then we'll get you back on the couch."

It was difficult to get her off of the floor. She couldn't help herself, and the satin dress was slippery in our hands. But finally we got her on the sofa.

We were all out of breath but giggling—even Lana.

"What's going on? I heard you laughing before I came in the house." Grandma had arrived. Then she saw Lana in the dress. "Have you been up?" she asked.

"Yeah," Lana sort of wheezed, leaning back against the pillows. "We danced."

Grandma's mouth tightened, but she didn't say anything. She took off her coat and went to the kitchen. "Get Lana out of her dress while I make some hot chocolate to go with the cookies I brought."

It was harder to get the dress off than it had been to put it on, and she slumped on the couch. Andy had to hold the cup to her mouth.

Shortly thereafter Grandma sent us away so that Lana could nap.

Outside Shoua and I smiled at each other. "She danced," we said.

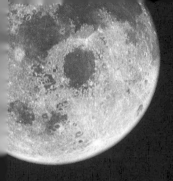

12. Moon of the Terrible

January was so cold, and then we had sudden warmth—a Chinook wind that eased the chill. Maybe it was the wind that took Lana away from the cold, or maybe she didn't dance long enough, but she didn't have the time to try again.

The night before the funeral there was a wake service at St. Matthew's Church. As the casket was brought in, Shoua and her parents came to Grandma. They handed her the quilt that she had given Shoua when we adopted her.

"Please cover Lana with this beautiful blanket as our farewell present. We would be honored."

The hall was full of family as well as kids and teachers from school. Mr. Richard gave Shoua and me hugs.

"Lana was a great gal. You were lucky to have her for your friend."

"Sister," both Shoua and I said, correcting him.

After the prayers Father Jim said, "Lana was the first girl acolyte at St. Matthew's. She was very proud to be an acolyte and especially to carry the cross in the procession. But she always wished that she could sing in the choir like Lori did. 'Why does she have a pretty voice, and I sound like a frog?' she asked me once. I told her that she had her own gifts and that she was the best acolyte I'd ever had." He smiled, "Even though sometimes she skipped in time to the hymns.

"Now, we're sad that such a lovely, talented girl has left us, but I hope some of you"—he motioned to the people—"will share your memories of Lana."

The hall was quiet, but then one of Lana's teachers said, "She was always in a hurry. She would run when she should have walked."

Another said, "Lana always wanted to be the first to do something. Not necessarily be first to get a good grade, which she got if she wanted to—but there were so many other things she rushed to do. I used to tell her to slow down, that she had lots of time."

"Lana was proud of her American Indian heritage. She made sure that we all knew she was Lakota," a classmate said.

Andy stood up. "One time when were younger—when she was taller than me—two guys picked on me. They didn't get far, because out of nowhere came Lana! She punched them out! She wasn't afraid of anything." He sat down and put his head in his hands.

Shoua spoke next, with tears running down her face. "Lana wanted Lori, her, and me to be blood sisters so that I could be an Indian.

"She was full of mischief." She told about swiping watermelon and the *chichi* in the attic. "She was my friend and my sister."

I laughed and cried at the same time as I listened to the others. Then I told about Lana in the floating cooler. "After that, she was so nice to me—she thought I'd saved her life. But I couldn't do that."

On the way home the wind whipped around the corner of the house, sending stinging snow into our faces. The Chinook winds were gone.

"Too cold," I said. I shivered and realized that this was Moon of the Terrible.

Aunt Martha found Lana's calendar. Lana hadn't written the Lakota names—just as I knew she wouldn't—but had made pictures to illustrate the moons, and she had given her own names to the months that showed what important event had happened to her.

We could tell that she had taken more time with the first pictures she drew. They had more color and detail. Many were cut and pasted on construction paper. Then she used the computer, copying the same clouds, the same moon. It was a quicker way to do it, and she had finished the twelve months.

Oh, I wished I could take back all of the mean things I'd said—all the jealous thoughts about her showing off and wanting to be the best. I turned the pages of her calendar, recognizing that the pictures were better than the carefully printed words I'd written for each month.

Christmas vacation was over. I could stay at home by myself after school—Grandpa and Grandpa no longer had to watch me.

Then Shoua and her family came to say goodbye.

"My uncle found a job for Dad, and we can live with him until we find a place in Minneapolis. We'll be with family again." Tears rolled down her cheeks, and I wept with her.

Mr. Vang told Grandpa, "We are forever grateful that you made us part of your family. We—I—will miss you."

We hugged Shoua and wept until Grandma said, "We'll always have a place for you, your mother, and your father in our family. But it's best that you be with your own family."

I kept busy with schoolwork, and Mom urged me to make new friends. I tried, but it didn't work even though I hated the quiet of being alone.

One day Grandma called and asked, "Lori, can you come over to stay with Chuckie after school tomorrow? Grandpa and I have an appointment."

Grandpa picked us up after school. "It sure is quiet at our house with just Chuckie there," he said. "It would be good if you would come over at least once a week to play with him."

Chuckie was waiting for us at the house. "Lori!" He jumped up and down, excited to see me.

I hugged him and then heard, "Hi, Lori," and looked up to see Andy sitting on the couch.

"What are you doing here?" I asked.

"He comes to play with Chuckie at least once a week," Grandma explained.

I felt guilty. I should have been doing that; Chuckie was lonely, too.

Chuckie took our hands. "Want to play?" he asked.

We played cars and soldiers and read *Dancing Tepees*. He carefully studied each picture. "Lana made good pictures, too," he said.

Then we went out to play in the snow.

"Remember when we made tracks?" Chuckie asked. I nodded, trying not to let him see my tears. "Let's make new tracks," he said.

He followed Andy and me carefully, stepping in the same tracks, so that it looked like only one person was walking in the snow.

"Now look," he said and pointed. "The tracks will melt and be gone. Lana made the first tracks, and so they're under ours. Lana said that even if we can't see them anymore, they'd always be there. Is that right, Lori?" He looked up at me, and I saw the doubt in his eyes.

I squeezed his hand and answered, "Yes, they'll always be there."

University of Nebraska Press

Also of Interest by Virginia Driving Hawk Sneve:

Grandpa Was a Cowboy and an Indian and Other Stories

"'Grandpa,' I quietly asked, 'how come when you talk about the past, you say you were a cowboy and an Indian?' I sensed the regret in his short laugh when he answered, 'Cause I was both and both ways are gone forever.'" With great imagination and vigor, awardwinning Lakota storyteller Virginia Driving Hawk Sneve treats readers to a collection of her best stories.

ISBN: 978-0-8032-9300-7 (paper)

The Trickster and the Troll

The friendship and adventures of Iktomi, the trickster figure from Lakota legend, and Troll, the familiar character from Norse mythology, are the subject of this imaginative, marvelously spun tale. While searching for his Norwegian immigrant family, the gentle, lumbering Troll meets Iktomi. The vain, opportunistic Trickster soon discovers that he too has lost his people, the Lakota. When Iktomi and Troll eventually find their peoples, they are neither recognized nor wanted. The lonely Trickster and the Troll find solace in their friendship and take refuge in a cave. Many years pass before they are discovered and loved again.

ISBN: 978-0-8032-9263-5 (paper)

Order online at www.nebraskapress.unl.edu or call 1-800-755-1105. Mention the code "BOFOX" to receive a 20% discount.